INSTAFAMOUS

ALSO BY ERIKA J. KENDRICK

Cookie Monsters

Squad Goals

INSTAFAMOUS

ERIKA J. KENDRICK

LB
LITTLE, BROWN AND COMPANY
New York Boston

Interior design by Michelle Gengaro-Kokmen.

Interior art credits: Microphone © lesyau_art/Shutterstock.com;
Social Media Icons © macrojobs/Shutterstock.com;
Musical Notes © Cosmic_Design/Shutterstock.com;
Monster Emoji © Cosmic_Design/Shutterstock.com;
Exploding-head Emoji © Valentina Vectors/Shutterstock.com

Little, Brown and Company
Hachette Book Group
1290 Avenue of the Americas, New York, NY 10104
Visit us at LBYR.com

First Edition: October 2024

Library of Congress Cataloging-in-Publication Data

Names: Kendrick, Erika J., author.
Title: Instafamous / Erika J. Kendrick.
Description: First edition. | New York : Little, Brown and Company, 2024. | Audience: Ages 8–12. | Summary: "A middle school diva's hunt for the spotlight speaks to the importance of friendship, family, and mental fitness—even in the midst of fame"—Provided by publisher.
Identifiers: LCCN 2023050648 | ISBN 9780316566025 (hardcover) | ISBN 9780316566056 (ebook)
Subjects: CYAC: Theater—Fiction. | Social media—Fiction. | Mental health—Fiction. | Best friends—Fiction. | Friendship—Fiction. | Middle schools—Fiction. | Schools—Fiction. | Celebrities—Fiction. | African Americans—Fiction.
Classification: LCC PZ7.1.K476 In 2024 | DDC [Fic]—dc23
LC record available at https://lccn.loc.gov/2023050648

ISBNs: 978-0-316-56602-5 (hardcover), 978-0-316-56605-6 (ebook)

Printed in Indiana, USA

LSC-C

Printing 1, 2024

To all the dreamers who embrace the magic of possibility

CHAPTER 1

"I am destined to be a star."

I shove my big blond curls into a tattered scrunchie and stare at the determined girl in the mirror. I exhale, narrowing my eyes at the chalky green mask on my very beige skin. I can still see the dotty freckles hanging out around my nose. I lower the volume on the radio and repeat the affirmation, only louder this time.

"I am DESTINED to be a STAR."

I pick at the clay on my dimpled chin before taking a step back to square my shoulders in the mirror. Running through the vocal scales, exercising my larynx, I tighten my core, then hit that tricky high note like my bestie in my mind, Ariana Grande. Then, for good luck, I repeat one last time, "I AM DESTINED—"

"Boogie! Get in the shower," Mom howls at me from the bottom of the stairs. "Manifest your dreams after you eat your waffles."

She doesn't get it; she's already a star. But I keep explaining to her that it's my time to shine. I'm twelve and anxious to follow in her footsteps, for crying out loud. I mean, c'mon, I'm only the best singer in Santa Monica under twenty. My mom is way over twenty, so she doesn't count, but my time is now! It's in my genes, threaded into my DNA, bursting at the seams.

I take another deep breath and repeat my truth. "I am already a star. The world just needs to hurry and catch up." Okay, so maybe I remixed the affirming words a little, but today's vibe is all about making magic happen.

I shake the tension from my shoulders and lean closer to the mirror. I point my blingy press-on nails at my face that's feeling tighter by the second and sing my scales again. I grab my hairbrush and belt out three different harmonies spanning the octave.

"LYRIC WHITNEY HOUSTON DARBY!"

I crack open the door, careful not to let the steam

escape. It's my secret sauce, the other part of my skin hack that keeps my pores perfect. "You can't rush the pretty, Mom!"

"I have to be at the studio in twenty minutes. If you're not downstairs, you can walk all that pretty to school by yourself."

I blast the radio that's been looping commercials about the new Parker Hotel around the corner. "Ugh!" I sigh, hopping into the shower and grabbing my exfoliating loofah. "Come on already! Make the big announcement!"

And just as I'm hitting my armpits with the world's sweetest lavender wash, it happens. Right then. Right there.

"Boogie!"

"It's happening, Mom! It's actually happening!"

I slip and slide around the bathtub before almost ripping the shower curtain apart. Fumbling with the volume on the radio, I scream, just as the morning DJ explains it all.

"That's right, Los Angeles, you heard me. Everyone's favorite TV show, *American Rockstar,* is finally coming to LA to find the newest, hottest, biggest voice! We all know that LA singers have the pipes to blow every other city out of the water. So, if you're at least twelve years old with industry experience, come on down to the Pier in Santa Monica next Saturday and see if you've got what it takes to be the next American Rockstar."

I grab my towel and race from the bathroom, soap suds flying into the ceiling fan, and bolt downstairs to the kitchen.

"Mom! Mom!" I yell at her, trying to catch my breath. "It's happening. It's finally my turn."

"Boogie, what are you talking about now? I have to leave the house in ten and you have soap in your nostrils."

"*Rockstar,* Mom! It's coming to Santa Monica, and this year I'm old enough to compete for the big singing contract. A real live record deal. For me."

Mom slides her arms into her pink-and-gold sequined jacket. I've been eyeing it for two whole months. Then she whirls her arms around her long, coily hair. "Not that God-awful TV show that exploits all those young kids and puts them in contracts that last until way after they're dead and buried."

"Mommmmmmm! Très harsh. And so not true."

"I'm sorry, Boogie; I know you've had your heart set on being on that show since you were seven, but it's just not the best thing for you." She kisses my cheek and rubs it in with her thumb. "Mommy knows what's best for you and your career."

"But I don't haaavvve a career," I huff back at her, pulling the towel up to my collarbone as a tiny puddle of swampy suds forms around my feet. "At least this way, I can finally start one. It would be in front of millions of people who'd surely fall in love with me. I mean, look at me." I twirl in front of the refrigerator and pucker into a series of red-carpet smooches. "I'm already a total star. The world just doesn't know it yet."

"Yes, Boogie, you are. But we've talked about this. *American Rockstar* is not the smartest way to launch your magnificent voice into the world. I have a different plan for my sweet, spunky, talented girl."

"But you always say that. When is this life-changing plan going to start?"

"You have to be patient, honey. These things take time and very careful planning. You need the right agent. And manager. And publicist. And—" She shrugs into a sigh. "Besides, I thought you were going to do your first musical this year. What are they doing again?" I watch Mom fold her arms over her slouchy graphic tee and bite into her lip. "*Annie*? *Bye Bye Birdie*? Oh no, wait... it's *Godspell*, right?"

I bite into my lip, too, but instead of crossing my arms to mirror hers, I shove my hands into my hips and grunt, "*The Wiz*! Who cares about Emerald City when the Pier will be calling my name on Saturday?!"

Mom pushes a plate of cold waffles and runny eggs at me. "Here, Boogie. Eat. And why aren't you losing your marbles over *The Wiz*? It produced 'Home,' our signature song."

"But it isn't *American Rockstar*. And besides, I can sing our signature song for the producers at auditions next Saturday."

"Sorry, Lyric; the answer is no. Now, I have to dash, and you need food to get you through your manic Monday." She grabs her oversize sunnies and designer backpack and heads for the front door.

"Uh, Mom, aren't you forgetting something?" I close my eyes and tilt my head for her legendary sugar.

"Yes, of course. What was I thinking?" She doubles back, taking her thermos from the kitchen island, and hightails it toward the front door. "What would I do without you?"

"Are you kidding me?!" I yell into the air, hopping onto the island to get a good look at the woman who normally makes me happier than any other human on the planet. This morning, however, is definitely an exception. Still, I need a few Jade Darby smooches to get this already disappointing day started.

"Now you know I'm only teasing you." She dances back

to me and slobbers my whole face with her delightfully wet kisses. Then she breaks into our signature song.

♪♪ *When I think of home, I think of a place...*

And right on cue, I join her.

Where there's love overflowing.

"You two should really record an album," my dad says, rushing into the kitchen to join us. He takes a bite of my greenish-yellow eggs. Then, on second thought, he spits them out into the trash can at the end of the island. He hides his very blue eyes and makes the quintessential *ick* face.

"Elvis!"

Very little gets past Mom. Over the years, Dad has learned to pretend that her cooking is top-notch. Still, the two of us know Mom could easily be cast on one of those shows about horrible cooks. She'd win, too. A total shoo-in. But let's be honest, with her hypnotic voice, she doesn't need to know how to throw down in the kitchen. Period.

"Is that duet album in the works yet?" Dad kisses my

forehead and squeezes my cheeks. I watch as he beams with dad-pride and tugs on his salt-and-pepper goatee.

"Oh, Elvis, you've been saying that since we brought her home from the hospital and she screamed her head off for three whole weeks."

"And I still mean it today. I don't know, Jade, our little one just might have a bigger voice than yours."

"Well, she got it naturally, that's for sure," Mom says, as she sneakily slides around Dad's butt to peek into the trash can. She pokes him in his ribs when she sees his food splattered over the cereal box, giving Tony the Tiger's face a pukey green makeover.

Dad forces a ridiculous smile, but Mom just rolls her eyes at him and asks, "Did she tell you that she's going to showcase that voice on the big stage at Valentine Middle?"

"This year, they're doing *The Wiz*," my aunt Jackie's voice croaks from behind my dad. We all turn around and watch her, shuffling her pristine slippers into the kitchen, her morning wig tattered around the edges. "Isn't that what I read in the Santa Monica newspaper?"

"Morning, Auntie," Mom says to her mother's oldest sister, who lives with us. Aunt Jackie is hovering somewhere around eighty years old, but she says she lost count "many moons ago."

"Morning?" Aunt Jackie scoffs, pointing her cane

at the wall clock that hasn't worked in almost a year. "Morning started four hours ago when I got up. It's almost dinnertime."

"Aw, Boogie," Dad gushes, as Aunt Jackie scuffles over to me. She stops to check out the eggs that are stinking up the trash. "You'll be the best Dorothy Santa Monica has ever seen," he says.

Aunt Jackie sneaks me a Werther's candy from her red housecoat and whisper-explains, "You'll be hungry later."

"But, Dad," I say, taking the candy, "I was telling Mom that next Saturday at the Pier, they're having auditions for—"

"Elvis, we're going to be late," Mom interrupts, looping her arm through his. "The band already texted twice."

Dad high-fives me before turning to Mom with his usual gooey, gross grin. *Ugh!*

He adores her. Plain and simple. He's been smitten ever since they summered at music camp in high school. I can't blame him either. Everything about Mom is epic—minus her cooking. But other than that... fareals EPIC! She recorded an album five years ago and one of the singles, "Paper Cuts," went platinum. She was on every late-night talk show singing her heart out, and Dad was right there holding her down, playing the drums in their band: Love, Jade. He's been by her side the last five years while she toured the world singing that chart-topping bop. Some people call her a one-hit wonder, but she gets really annoyed when they do. So I don't. Unless I'm mad at her for not taking my career seriously.

"See you after school, Boogie. I made sure to schedule our studio time around you this week. I meant what I said about making time for both your little and big moments."

I can't hide the grin that's oozing gratitude all over my uber-tight skin.

She narrows her eyes to show she means serious business. "But don't you forget to sign up for auditions."

I cross my fingers behind my back. "For *American Rockstar*?"

Mom shoots me her best grimace. "Your dad is right; you'll make a fabulous Dorothy."

I watch as they walk out the front door, my smile fading into the silence.

But I'm an American Rockstar.

CHAPTER 2

Later that morning, I schlep to my locker at school and slurp my venti coffee, feeling the electric energy around me. Usually Mondays at Valentine Middle are pretty mundane, but today the hallway is buzzing about the latest and greatest that's going down this Thursday.

"Lyric!" Georgia shoves a bunch of gym clothes, a big denim jacket, and four hard textbooks into the locker beside me. I watch her struggle to shut the door. She gives up, and a spiral notebook tumbles out and smushes the top of the cowboy hat on her head. "Where have you been all morning? I was waiting and waiting...and then still waiting for you by the sign-up sheet outside the theater."

"Take a deep breath and slow down." I rub her shoulders with my fingertips, but that's no match for her high-octane enthusiasm right now.

She takes off her cowboy hat, punches out its dents, and then ruffles her matted bangs. "But you don't understand. I had to sign you up for auditions when I saw *her* scribble *her* name first."

I can feel the tulle ruffles on my midi tutu shifting. "You did what? And who scribbled whose name?" I shake my butt until the tiered ruffles settle into place.

"I started to sign you up for Thursday's big auditions. And *her* is the one and only Stormy Jackson. She's totally trying out for Dorothy, and she already thinks she's going to get the part. I had to show her that she's not the only big voice on the West Coast."

"No worries. I signed you up. But you do know that she's Michael Jackson's niece, twice removed, on his mother's side," Twinkie explains as she joins us, completely consumed by what's happening on her phone.

Georgia Reign and Saanvi Patel (aka Twinkie) are a few of my absolute faves from elementary. They've been two of the loudest members on my support squad since we were in the third-grade choir. We performed a few songs from *Peter Pan*. Fact: I completely crushed my Tinkerbell solo. Ever since that showstopping performance, they've been rooting for me to blow up and get my own reality show, outfitted with a glam makeup artist and stylist. I keep explaining that I'm already super fly and don't need a stylist. An agent and a manager, though... yes, please. Sign me up already!

"Wait." Georgia taps her cowgirl heel into the floor. "Is she really related to the King of Pop, or does she just go around town using that last name to get into concerts?" Then she shrugs. "I guess it doesn't really matter either way; you're the real deal, L-Boogie."

See, that's what I'm saying. Georgia and Twinkie only want the best for me, just like I want for them. It's true boomerang love. We make great locker mates and an overall groovy trio, each bringing our own vibe to the middle school party. Twinkie might be textbook, introvert-shy, but she's a wiz with that pen. The girl can write like nobody's business. She even won a few competitions for her short stories. Georgia, on the other hand, is an even bigger ham than me. She always says school isn't really her thing, and if her daily dose of detentions is any indication, she's right about that—and on track for being awarded the most detentions this whole semester. When she isn't on punishment (but she always is), she's auditioning around town for stuff. She has the acting bug. Bad. Good thing, too, because she got kicked out of choir for pulling a legendary prank on Gia Carlyle, one of the not-so-nice girls in elementary. She always said it gave her more time to explore her true love: the stage.

"Stormy even had the nerve to say that she's entitled to the role of Dorothy because Michael Jackson already played in the TV version like a zillllion years ago and something about it being her birthright." Georgia changes the lock on her locker like she does every month. She's superstitious and more than a little paranoid. "Can you believe that? A total clout chaser."

"We are *nawt* going to make this whole morning all about Stormy," Twinkie says, shoving her tiny head into her locker on the other side of me. Her long braid, embellished with beautiful Indian jewelry, hangs past the belt buckle on her denim overalls. I try to catch a few words, but her muffled voice only strings syllables through the air. Then she pops her head out to clearly declare, "Everybody just needs to get in formation. It's all about L-Boogie this year. Right, Lyric?"

I nod in agreement even though they have no idea what I'm secretly planning.

"It's about time a school musical came along so you

can show them all what you're working with." Georgia nibbles on her nails and then points her finger in the air for emphasis. With her other hand, she pops the collar on her red-and-green flannel shirt and nods at me. "You're a SE-RI-OUS superstar."

This year, both my girls are on the same page as Mom. They're determined to have me on that stage with Toto, the Tin Man, and all the Munchkins. See, Valentine Middle isn't all about the musicals. They usually put on some big play that has barely any music in it, if at all. So there haven't been any juicy songs to sink my teeth into. But now we finally have a musical worthy of my chops, and all I can think about is *American Rockstar.* Twinkie and G think Dorothy will single-handedly jump-start my high school singing career. But who cares about high school when all I can think about is national television!

"Stormy can have that part," I say, matter-of-fact. "I'm not interested."

Twinkie grabs her neck and gasps for air. "Whaddo you mean, Lyric?"

"This could be the big start of it all." Georgia cocks her head to the side as if it'll help her understand. "In three more semesters, we'll be in high school."

Twinkie stands on her tiptoes to look me square in the

eye. "And the more musicals and talent shows you do now, the sooner you'll blow up at Valentine High. That was always our plan."

"Well... plans can change." I turn away from them and open my locker to grab my English book and vintage Trapper Keeper. "And sometimes you have to make room for a new plan."

Twinkie leans in and grins, grabbing her earlobes. "I'm all ears. I like where this is going already."

"I'm lost." Georgia's brows dip into her forehead. "Where the heck *is* this going besides to the big auditions on Thursday?"

"I have no idea." Twinkie pulls out her smartphone, presses RECORD, and points it at my perfectly glossed lips. "But I love when Lyric gets that look on her face. It means Valentine Middle better get ready for something bi-ig."

I snatch her phone and dead the Live before looping my arms through both Georgia's and Twinkie's.

"Dish the deets." Twinkie nudges me as we turn to head into Mr. Reynolds's English class. "I'll need to get everything ready for you."

"I only have two words."

"*THE. WIZ*!" Georgia exclaims. "Why are we dancing around the obvious? It's your big moment."

"See, Georgia," I say, sliding into my desk in the middle

of the classroom. I fluff my skirt's ruffles and explain, "I *am* the moment. Wherever I go. You seem to keep forgetting that."

"You sure are." Twinkie gushes over me, straightening my vegan leather vest that's hanging coolly over my crisp white tank. "And I'm totes here for it."

"Thank you, Twinkie." I hold my head toward the heavens and wait for the anticipation to build like only a true star would. Then... I announce, *"American. Rockstar."*

"Whoa!" The phone slips from Twinkie's grip and drops onto the desk. "That's the big singing competition with all the teenagers who want to become famous superstars and—"

"Ohhhhh, now I get it!" Georgia grins. "I see what you did there."

"Why didn't I think of that? Of course you'll crush that show." Twinkie claps her hands in double time. "You're twelve now, so you can compete." She shakes her head in awe. "And you're absolutely perfect."

I sit back into my seat and cross my legs, allowing my suede booties to dangle at my bare ankles. "Stop." I blush, holding my hand up. Then I flip my fingers around, fanning my hand toward me for her to continue. "Keep going."

We all giggle until Georgia stops. I can see the light bulb flashing over her head.

"Wait a minute. Just one minute. Cuz I'm pretty sure that..." Georgia rummages through her cluttered backpack, dumping half the contents onto the floor beside her desk, until she finds her iPad. Twinkie and I watch her swipe through several screen pages until she lands on what she wants. "It says right here on their website that you need performing arts or industry experience to be considered for that show."

I twist my face into a frown and think deeply about that one little pesky detail.

Twinkie looks over Georgia's shoulder and points to the qualifying rules. "Yeah, she's right. It says it right here." She makes air quotes when she says, "Industry. Experience."

A few seconds pass before they both freeze, staring at me with the only obvious answer.

Twinkie doesn't bother to even blink. "IF you did the play, THEN you'd have performing arts experience. I don't think doing *Peter Pan* in elementary would count."

She's right. As an aspiring singing superstar, I get that I should have been doing musicals in any and everything south of Bakersfield. But the honest answer is that I'd rather be in the studio with Jade Darby and her band, learning from a pro. Working with kids who struggle to find their pitch is just not my jam. But now, I'm clearly going to have to make up for lost time.

"We were just kids, so I know there's no way they would count it," I hear Georgia saying about our time together in *Peter Pan*. "But *The Wiz* makes so much sense. Easy peasy." She stomps her boots into the linoleum floor. "Good thing you already signed her up."

"It's sorta my job as her agent and manager," Twinkie declares. "Duh."

I slouch into my seat and bite my bottom lip. This is quickly turning into a bigger scheme than I thought.

"And you know I find my entire life on that stage, so I'll be right next to you doing the play. I mean, I'm only going to make the dopest scarecrow!" Georgia exclaims, then she shrugs. "Everyone thinks I don't have a brain anyway."

"You're smart, G. Stop that." I put my hand over hers. "You just need to learn how to focus."

Twinkie points to the big heap of clutter on the floor beside Georgia's desk. "And maybe get organized."

"Yeah, yeah. I know. And I should probs stop ditching tutoring, so I don't fail every class except English," Georgia adds, shrinking into her seat. "It's just so hard for me to sit still while some math geek talks to me about probability. Blahhhhh!"

I squeeze her hand and state the truth. "That's how you'll finally get off punishment."

"I'm pretty sure the parentals will set me free to do something academic like the musical. They love a good extracurricular, and even they know all the greats got their start in school musicals."

Twinkie slides into the desk beside me, ready to take down the list of names. "Who, Georgia?"

"Well, I mean there was . . . well, there was . . . but then, there was . . ."

I watch Mr. Reynolds scribble stuff on the board. "If we're talking about the Broadway stage . . . well, there was Nick Jonas, Anna Kendrick, Ariana—"

"As in Grande?" Twinkie peps. "You, like, lurvvvve her."

"She *is* the ultimate. And I'm just like her. Except I'm mixed. You know, Elvis is white and Jade is Black. But that's just a tiny technicality."

"So . . . are we doing this spring musical thing?" Georgia asks, popping a piece of watermelon bubble gum into her mouth. "Twinkie, join us. We all know you have that amazy voice buried under all that scaredy-cat stuff you feel whenever you sing in public. We've all heard you in the shower at every sleepover since our third-grade trip to Beale Street in Memphis."

"Even though you always scampered to the back row in choir and hid behind Capricorn Reese, your voice was un-DE-niable."

Twinkie shakes her head so hard I think her neck is going to break. "And get up there in front of all those people in the theater? Nope, soooo nawt my thing."

"It'll just be us at the auditions, Twinkie," I explain as her left eye starts to twitch.

Georgia snuffles a giggle before it can escape. "I mean...you're a total lion. That scaredy-cat role is a perfect fit for you."

Twinkie ignores her, never taking her eyes off me. "Seriously, Lyric? Does it mean that much to you?"

"It would make it better to have my girls there. But if you don't want to"—I soothe, even though I know she just needs a friendly nudge—"I don't want to push you. BUT challenging ourselves is how we grow."

"I mean...if you really need me, I can be there," Twinkie's other eye starts to twitch, and she chokes on all the air around us. "I'm fine. Really. Let's do this."

"Okay then." I inhale deception—and exhale the perfect strategic plan. "Now. You all have to agree to do one more itty-bitty, teeny-weeny thing for me."

"Any. Thing. F-f-for you," Twinkie states, still struggling to catch her breath.

Georgia rifles through her backpack before turning it upside down and dumping the other half of her stuff onto the floor. "Don't mind me. I'm here for it, whatever it is. Y'all know I love a good plot twist."

"My mom can't know. She's not into *Rockstar*. Like, at all." I glance at Mr. Reynolds, who's frowning at the mess Georgia's made in the middle of his classroom. "The one and only Jade Darby said it's not a good fit for me and my career."

"But won't you get in trouble?" Twinkie asks, her brows dancing.

Georgia laughs. She does that sometimes. She thinks adults are just tall kids and that they're not always the smartest in the room. This time, I agree with her, especially when she says, "She does know that it'll give you way more exposure than Valentine Middle's production of *The Wiz*, doesn't she?"

"She has her own plan for me, but who knows when it'll happen. She just keeps saying that I'm not ready yet, while still promising to introduce me to talent agents and managers. But do you see me represented by some hotshot agency in Beverly Hills yet?"

When they don't answer, I yell, "Nope!"

Mr. Reynolds shifts his focus to me, and I pretend to

check out the words on his dry-erase board. But then, they quickly come into focus when I see:

THE WIZ
AUDITIONS THIS THURSDAY AFTER SCHOOL
THE THEATER
Director: Mr. Reynolds

I cross my arms over my vest and turn to my girls. "If Dorothy will get me on *American Rockstar*, then it's time to take an Uber to Kansas."

Georgia raises her fist in solidarity and pronounces, "To making you a star!"

Twinkie scoots her desk closer and takes several pics of me with her phone.

It's now or never, I think as I pose and pucker for my theater squad. They both giggle and say, "The star we know you already are."

CHAPTER 3

I spent the last two days counting down to Wednesday, the day I'm finally in my fave happy place: the studio!

I still pinch myself that I get to watch THE Jade Darby in the recording booth doing her thing, making the singing ancestors proud. Rudy, the sound engineer, twists a few knobs and adjusts a couple levels on the sound board, but that's mostly it. He's stroking his salt-and-pepper beard, flinging his half-up half-down man bun, bobbing his head to the beat of Jade Darby's next big hit, "Maserati Clouds." He leans all the way back in his swivel chair and throws his hands in the air. "Jade! You've never sounded better!"

I absolutely, wholeheartedly agree!

I slurp my caramel macchiato and look around at the instruments leaning against the padded wall that's been painted a deep, bold red. I scoot to the edge of the distressed orange leather sofa, close my eyes, and listen to her velvety voice do things that only great vocalists have done. Her ridiculous range sends me soaring, and I imagine a party in heaven where Aretha Franklin is the host and she's gossiping about Mom's big voice back here on earth.

"What's it like living with Jade Darby?" Rudy asks, snapping me back into the room. That's when I hear a few sniffles, but there's no one else in the room.

Is he crying?!

I peek open one eye and see Mom pointing at me, this time hitting a note that rivals Ariana Grande.

"Amazing," I answer Rudy, completely mesmerized as I watch Mom finish her song, take off her headphones, and balance them on the mic stand.

"How was that?" she asks, rounding the small corner to stand in the doorway.

"You're fabulous," Rudy says. "I'll mix it down, but to

be honest, there's not much that needs to be done. You did all the work for me."

"This voice is the gift that keeps on giving," Mom tells him as he grabs his keys and leaves, dabbing his eyes with the back of his shirtsleeve.

"So, what'd you think, Boogie?" Mom grabs a towel from a small stack on the end table.

"What Rudy said. Fabulous!" I gush, watching her hit the tiny sweat beads on her temples. "And I want to be just like you." I toss my coffee cup into the wastebasket and step over it so I can stand right next to her. She's only a few inches taller than me at this point, but I look all the way up to her. "One day, I want to be in there with you."

"Oh, it'll happen, Boogie," she says, matter-of-fact. "That voice is going to take you all around the world."

"Like yours does for you and Dad."

Mom plops down on the old couch and sinks into it. "Just like in your wildest dreams."

"Did you always see you and Dad traveling the world hitting all the stages together?"

Mom laughs, and I can't help but notice the glint in her eyes. "When I met your dad at music camp back in Chicago, he told me that he would be the luckiest guy if he could back me up for the rest of his life."

"That completely sounds like Dad." I laugh with her.

"He was set on chasing me all over the world if he had to. Music was our dream, and he was willing to do whatever he needed to make it all come true." Her head tilts to the ceiling and her brows crease. "I didn't see it."

"He knew he was so lucky to have crossed paths with Jade Darby, even way back then."

"No, Boogie." She smiles with her eyes this time. "He gave me you, so I was the lucky one."

I plop down on the couch beside her and scoot as close as I physically can to her.

"So," she says, turning her shoulder so she can face me. "Is there anyone new hanging around, waiting to chase you around the world?"

"Mom!"

"What? I'm just asking. Is it still... What's his name? Wait. It's coming to me." I watch Mom close her eyes and wave her fingers in the air like she's performing a magic trick.

"It's almost there. His name is..."

"MOM!"

"Almost got it.... It's... Arlo Sampson." She opens her eyes, and my cheeks are burning.

"STAWP!"

She's cheesing hard, and that only makes me blush harder.

"He is so ca-yoot, Boogie. In that old-school Johnny Depp mixed with Idris sort of way." She winks at me, and I cringe. "You've got good taste, that's for sure."

"MAWM!" I try hiding my face. "Are you seriously doing this to me right now?"

"What am I doing? I see you batting those long lashes whenever he picks Stella Rose up from scout meetings. You're a smitten kitten. It's sooo obvi."

"Don't talk like that." I shake my head. "Puh-leeez."

"Like what?"

"Like you're twelve!"

She reaches over me and digs into my rib cage. Her tickles make me heave.

"You're . . . you're . . . you're canceled!" I yell out to her.

This only makes her tickle me harder. And faster.

I'm out of breath when I yell at her, "Why are you like this?!"

Mom finally gives me a break and I manage to sit up straight, unzipping my hot pink puffy vest.

"That's my Boogie. Always my favorite girl."

"Am I?" I focus to make sure she means it.

"Forever," she says, grabbing the back of my head to pull me closer so she can plant a wet kiss on my forehead.

"Well, I guess . . ." I shut my eyes and blurt out, "The answer is yes."

"I knew it! I knew it! Arlo and Boogie sitting in a tree. K-I-S-S-I-"

"MAWMMM! OhMahGawd! Say less!"

Mom gets up from the couch and grabs a water from the mini fridge across the room. "You used to always tell me everything. We were inseparable just a few years ago, gossiping about the ins and outs of Valentine Elementary." She pushes her shoulders back to boast, "I was your best friend."

She was. I let my guard down and admit to her, "I don't have room for boys right now. I'm all about my career."

"I see," Mom says, taking a big swig of the water.

"And I've made a big decision." I watch her nose crinkle and she studies me with quizzical eyes. It's at that very moment that I decide to only tell her half my plan. "I'm going to audition to be in *The Wiz*."

"Now that's news I can use," Mom says, wrapping her arms around me. "You're going to be fabulous. This is the start of something big."

I hear her exhale, getting lost in a deep sigh, and I *have* to ask because I *have* to know. "Did you dream of this, too, when you were my age? Being a star?"

She sets the bottle of water on the end table. "I need you to hear this clearly." She crouches in front of me so that we're eye level. Then she squeezes my knees. "I wish

I had your life when I was your age. All I wanted was to simply be . . . normal."

"What does that even mean? Normal is so—"

"Underrated."

She eases onto the couch and opens her arm so I can slink in and snuggle closer. "I don't think I've ever told you this before, but when I was growing up in Chicago, I was just like every other kid on my block."

I check out her glitter makeup with just the right amount of sparkle dabbed into the creases of her eyes. And her military boots over her acid-washed denim. And her oversize, vintage designer sunnies that sit atop her head, securing her thick, shiny coils. "Can't imagine."

"Yep. And it was perfect."

"Not boring?"

"I had cousins who were like sisters. And friends who were like cousins. I had teachers who liked me and neighbors who were nice to me."

I shrug. "Sounds fine, I guess."

"And then it all went away."

"What do you mean?"

She pulls me closer and nuzzles my hairline. "I guess you're old enough to hear this now."

"I thought you told me everything. We were best friends, remember."

"I was your best friend. You've always been my daughter. There's a diff."

"Seriously?"

"Okay. A difference." Her eyes scan the sound board as she thinks about what she's admitting. "I may have left some things out; I didn't want you to ever think badly of your grandma."

"Why would I do that? Grams was always so proud of me." I look up at Mom. "So she wasn't really proud of me?"

"Yes, Boogie, you were the light of her life." Mom takes a deep breath, and I can feel her heart stomping out her truth. "It was me she wasn't always so proud of. At least not until the night she heard me sing. It was Thanksgiving, at the annual family talent show."

There's a noticeable glimmer in her eyes when she says, "I was happy being Lauren Smith."

"So, Grandma didn't name you Jade?"

"Shhh, it's a stage name. But, yes, she gave it to me."

"And you didn't want it?"

"Let's just say I preferred to stay normal, boring Lauren." Mom closes her eyes and drifts far away. I'm guessing back to her old life. "I had really cool friends, Boogie. You would've liked them."

"Is that how you ended up in LA?"

"I was a little younger than you. Your grandma thought

we needed to be in Hollywood so all the big people could see me. Then my whole life became about finding me the right manager and then the perfect agent. I barely went to school because of all the classes that took time away from me performing for all the strangers or working on my craft."

"So, you were homeschooled?"

"Sure," says Mom, looking away. "I had dance classes and singing lessons and even theater camp."

"But no more friends, huh?"

"It was very lonely."

"But you got an agent and a manager, right? So there's that."

"Yes, but at what cost, Boogie?" She shifts me around to look at her. "I was always auditioning or in rehearsals or in front of a camera."

"But...like...is that so bad?"

"You try having a singing coach who smokes a pack of cigarettes every single lesson. Who feels the need to sing in your face so you can 'hear the tone.'"

We both fall into the couch cushions and spew.

I shove my hand over my mouth. "That's just...too much EW!"

"Right, sis!"

"Nope, not doing 'sis' with you either," I say to her,

making air quotes. I do my best to stay on track. "So, no birthday parties or class trips or graduation celebrations?"

Mom shakes her head.

"Aw, Mom. I'm sorry that happened to you." I think about all the special people in my world. "I don't know what I'd do without Georgia or Twinkie or Brooklyn or Stella Rose or Lucy or—"

"You're so lucky, Lyric. That's why I want you to wait on the whole career thing. I just want you to enjoy your life and being twelve for as long as you can."

"Because you love me." I reach up and kiss her cheek. "Lauren Smith."

"Forever."

CHAPTER 4

I wouldn't trade any of the time I got with Mom. It's always like riding a high frequency when I get to share soul space with her. That's what she calls it. But good gawd, with big goals in front of me, the end of the week started to look IN-TENSE. As soon as I got home from the studio, I had to shift gears and focus on my *Rockstar* auditions—and now *The Wiz*, too. Mom was right about enjoying being twelve, but for me, that still meant killing my *Rockstar* auditions so I can compete on TV. I practiced my audition song, "Home," nonstop. I practiced it so much that when I went to sleep that night, I was sing-mumbling the words in my pillow. Around 3:00 AM, I woke up belting out the lyrics in the middle of my bedroom. Yes! I was legit sleep-singing; apparently, that's a thing.

"Lyric!" Twinkie whisper-yells my name in Mr. Chang's math class Thursday morning, snapping me back to the numbers.

I look at her, and she's bobbing her ponytail back and forth at Mr. Chang.

"Oh, uh—" I stammer when I realize he's called my name to answer a question.

Mr. Chang stands in front of the room with his hands shoved into his khaki trousers. I can tell that he's growing more impatient with me by the nanosecond. "Lyric, we're waiting for you to talk us through this multi-step problem. Will you be joining us today? Before the bell rings?"

I look at the desk next to me for an assist from Georgia, but she's slouched in her seat with her chin buried in her denim button-up and her eyeballs fixated on a video game on her phone. Like always.

"Uh, well. Uh, let's see. If...uh...," I stammer, my mind racing in a zillion different directions. I hate when I don't have the answer; I'm usually focused and on top of my stuff in class.

Twinkie hacks up an imaginary hairball, causing me to look at her. She lowers her hand past her strawberry-patterned romper and points to the answer on our worksheet.

"Yes, Mr. Chang," I begin, squaring my shoulders and sitting straight. I remix the problem a bit and shoot him the answer. "If I'm getting paid fifty bucks a week to sing, plus three dollars in tips per gig, and I want to earn at least one hundred dollars..."

"Yes, Ms. Darby." He steps to the side so I can join him at the board. "Continue."

I stand and smooth my high-waisted white pleated skirt and prep to write out the inequality. The class watches, waiting for me to sink or swim. I can feel the cable-knit cricket sweater tighten around my rib cage, but I rip through the solutions with ease anyway. Rocking my schoolwork has never been an issue, but with auditions for *The Wiz* happening today and *American Rockstar* next Saturday, following along with Mr. Chang's mathematical line of thinking is proving to be exhausting.

Mr. Chang checks in with the class, who are all in agreement—except Georgia.

"Ms. Reign?" I race to my seat when Mr. Chang steps in front of his desk and narrows his eyes to focus on her. *Uh-oh.* "What do you think of Lyric's inequality and solution?"

My heart drops into my bobby socks when Georgia, completely clueless about Mr. Chang's questions, slams her phone onto her desk.

"Crud!" Georgia gripes into the air, having lost her bounty in her fave game.

"Ms. Reign! I'll need to see you after class."

"Huh?" she squeaks, turning to me. "What'd I do this time?"

I nod at the puzzle of numbers in front of Mr. Chang, but it's too late. Georgia's eyes dart around the classroom, settling on the REWARDS & CONSEQUENCES board hanging over the door.

"Detention today, Ms. Reign."

"Again!" Twinkie and I both yelp back at him this time.

"But... Mr. Chang! I have auditions today after school. I'm going to miss them if you make me go to detention."

"See me after, Ms. Reign," he says, just as the bell dismisses us from a world filled with boring babble about stuff that has NOTHING to do with singing.

The class files into the hallway, and I hang back with Twinkie while Georgia begs for her musical theater life.

"Do you think he's going to let her off the hook?" Twinkie asks as we pretend not to ear-hustle their convo.

"I dunno, but I do know who will understand our desperate little sitch," I say, grabbing Twinkie's hand and motoring out the door and around the corner to find Mr. Reynolds.

"What's up, ladies?" he asks when we stumble over each other to get to him.

"Georgia!" I yell, stomping my white chunky sneakers into the floor.

"Detention!" Twinkie adds.

"But... auditions!" I finish, out of breath.

And that's all we need to say for him to get that we need him to rescue her from the grips of after-school prison.

"What did she do this time?" our favorite teacher asks. See, the thing about Mr. Reynolds is that he's the one grown-up who just seems to get us. Georgia is no exception. He always understands her middle school monsters, even when they rear their messy heads in his classroom.

Mr. Reynolds grabs his backpack and locks his classroom for the day. "Okay. Let's see what we can do."

When we get back to Mr. Chang's room, Georgia is on the brink of tears.

"Mr. Chang, can I have a quick word?" is all we hear him say to our math teacher before Chang doubles back to Georgia and informs her that he'll need to have a conference with her parentals about her attention in class—or lack thereof.

"Okay," Georgia starts, her voice quivering. Whenever this happens, we all know that it's only a matter of minutes before she completely breaks and the waterfall of tears gushes all over our plans. "But—but can I still go to the audition today?"

"Mr. Reynolds has assured me, Ms. Reign, that this outlet might be just what you need to help you get and stay focused. He thinks you need a place to direct all your energy. Believe it or not, we all want you to win." He strokes the peach fuzz on his face and peers at Georgia. "Nevertheless, we must think about what's at the root of this. Your grades are suffering in my class, and your attention span needs some, well, attention. It's time to call your parents in for a conversation."

When he gives Georgia the green light to try out for the play, we trudge down the hall, heading for the theater. "Do you think they'll put you on punishment?" Twinkie asks as we round the corner and walk into the big room filled with kids.

Georgia fusses with her cowboy hat. "If they do, the play will have to stay in my rearview."

I toss my arm over Georgia's shoulder. "We should only think positive thoughts right now. We all have a big afternoon in front of us. She's going to be fine. We all are." I sure hope I'm right about this. Today is turning into a hodgepodge of uncertainty, and the only thing I know for sure is that I have to get cast in the musical to ensure that my career takes off. And I need both my girls by my side to step into my legacy.

Georgia doesn't say anything as we look around the theater, checking out all the frantic energy. She tugs on her suspenders, over and over again, until they finally snap.

"I need you to relax," I say, reaching for her hands. "It's all good, G."

"Duh. I'm trying," she snaps back. "Don't you think I know that?"

The thing about Georgia is she doesn't like being babied. She gets seriously bent out of shape if you treat her like a kid, even though she gets in trouble more than any of my other friends AND she's the youngest member of my entire school squad by a whole month. So, technically, she is the baby.

"Uh, this is legit a big deal. It looks like everyone at Valentine Middle came out to audition," Twinkie says, caught in her own spiderweb of nerves. "I thought the theater would be pretty empty."

"It'll be fine," I say, watching her eyes bulge and her hands start to shake. She's one of my friends who low-key panics whenever she presents in front of the class. The last time Twinkie struggled was in English when we were in the middle of our public-speaking assignment. We had to get up in front of everyone, and we weren't allowed to have partners. Twinkie begged Mr. Reynolds to let me present with her, but because it was an autobiographical piece, he wouldn't budge. We were all proud of Twinkie for getting through it even though she was the very last kid to go on the very last day of speeches. She ended up getting a C- on the assignment, but we celebrated at the Cheesecake Factory anyway. Hey, sometimes getting through the challenge is the big win, and it absolutely deserves a slice of Oreo Dream cheesecake.

"So, you came after all," Stormy Jackson says, sashaying up to us in an outift that's probably an actual *Wizard of Oz* Halloween costume. I mean, she's wearing Dorothy's infamous blue-and-white checkered dress with the white puffy sleeves, and even the wood basket purse and matching sparkly red dance shoes. *This girl!*

"Of course she came," Georgia says, still trying to reattach her suspenders to her denim. "She's only the best singer in this entire school."

Stormy isn't intimidated at all by Georgia's gruff stance. Then when Georgia steps right into Stormy's personal space, Stormy doesn't even flinch.

"It's not like you don't know that I'm related to the King of Pop. There's no way I won't be the star of this show. This is the musical where he was the star during the Motown era, on television, in front of millionsssssss—in case you didn't know," she scoffs, rolling her beady eyes into the back of her head. We do our best to hold back laughter when she opens her backpack to reveal a red studded faux-leather biker jacket. "It's for good luck."

"It's... a jacket," I clarify, squinting at it, then back at her.

"No." She fluffs her curly afro puffs and clarifies. "It's an exact replica of the famous jacket *he* wore in one of his videos."

"You're so... so...," I blurt out, but then I catch myself.

Fun fact: I don't like being mean. I don't think mean girls are cool. At all. But Mom tells me I possess a streak that I need to keep in check, especially when I'm feeling threatened. Dad says to always turn the other cheek, but what does that even mean? How can I turn my cheeks? And which way am I supposed to be turning them? *Whatevs.* What I do know is that this girl has an unhealthy obsession with Michael Jackson, and no one has even been able to prove that she's actually part of his legendary family.

"She's Jade Darby's daughter!" Twinkie says, crossing her arms over her chest. "We can easily prove that with a phone call. Can you say the same?"

"Thespians! Thespians!" Winnie Walsh rolls up to us in her tricked-out wheelchair. "Save it for the stage," she orders, with pink and gold streamers hanging from her wheels for extra school spirit today. "I'm your stage manager, and right now the only thing we need is for you to sign in right here." She shoves a clipboard and Sharpie into Stormy's belly. "It's going to be a good battle of the big voices today, I see."

"You need a worthy opponent for a battle," Stormy says, scribbling her name on the pink sheet of lined paper. She draws a tiny heart next to her name, swivels on the soles of her shoes, and struts back to her seat in the front row.

"I wouldn't worry about her," Brooklyn Ace, one of my good friends from my scout squad, says over my shoulder. "You're a shoo-in! Trust. You're going to make our show so epic."

"Thanks, B!"

Brooklyn is my fave Valentine Middle HoneyBee cheerleader. She's also Valentine's phenomenal World Scouts cookie queen, but more importantly, she's one of my BFFs. Even though she's made it known that she's no singer, she texted me last night and promised to try out to be a Munchkin with the rest of the HoneyBee cheer-leaders if I was still planning to throw my hat in the ring for the part of Dorothy. I have one of the dopest support squads. Period.

Brooklyn unzips her red-and-white jogger jacket and looks around the theater. She untangles her rainbow goddess braids and points to the different clusters of kids waiting for auditions to begin. "The cheerleaders are over there, ready to learn the Munchkin dance routine." I notice that my Sunflower troopmates from the World Scouts are micromanaging the other stuff. Brooklyn continues breaking it down. "Stella Rose is handling set design with a few of the football players backstage, and Lucy is rifling through the costumes for the *Wiz* wardrobe closet. She's in charge of it this year," Brooklyn says, giving us the behind-the-scenes play-by-play.

It's even more encouraging to know that the rest of my scout squad is here, too.

We just finished our annual scout cookie competition a month ago, and now our friend group is tighter than ever. Even though B didn't win, Stella Rose, Lucy, and I had the best time deepening our sisterhood. Yeah, they're my girls. I make a mental note to bring cupcakes to our next troop meeting. My little delish way of saying thank you!

Twinkie shuffles her feet around in place. "I think I should probs be in the group over there with the set stuff.

I'm pretty sure I could build something and not have a panic attack. Maybe work on the yellow brick road. How hard could that be?"

"But you're a righteous singer with a velvety voice," I offer. "If I do say so myself."

Georgia squeezes Twinkie's shoulders to give her extra support. "Yeah, you're with us, friend. Right where you're supposed to be."

We all watch for a few seconds as Twinkie's eyes take turns twitching. First her left one then her right. Then her left one again.

"Take deep breaths," Brooklyn says, steadying herself. "Here. Watch me." Twinkie watches Brooklyn for a few secs, then imitates her when she grabs her ears and starts rubbing them like it'll make quarters tumble out. I don't dare laugh, though. Brooklyn has become somewhat of an anti-anxiety ambassador. She's like a superhero with all that mental fitness stuff she's learning in therapy.

While they work to nix their nerves, I check out the rest of the scene. Mr. Reynolds seems to be working overtime to wrangle all the kids. He palms his forehead and winces at the energy swelling in the audience before taking the stage with his microphone in hand.

"Okay, everyone. Let's settle down and get started. It's almost showtime."

One by one, the clusters of wannabe superstars quiet each other with a wave of "Shhhhhhhh" bouncing around the room.

"I'm excited to have you all here as we bring our best selves to the stage today. I am truly proud of each of you for showing up to put your talents on display. You should be proud for having the courage to even try out." Mr. Reynolds unloosens his checkered tie as the audience of students yells and screams in agreement. "Everyone won't see their name on the official cast list tomorrow, but I encourage you to meet me here next year to do it all over again. You deserve that."

"I don't have the luxury of waiting until next year," I whisper-fess to Georgia and Twinkie as we scoot into the row closest to the door. Stormy Jackson turns around and winces in our direction. "It's now or never for me."

"First up, performers, is Lyric Darby," Mr. Reynolds says, scanning the crowd for me.

"What happened to saving the best for last?" I ask, standing up.

"You're Lyric Whitney Houston Darby. Don't you forget it," Georgia says.

Twinkie stands and starts applauding. She winks at me and says, "Valentine Middle's very own rockstar."

And just like that, I remember why I'm even here: to be eligible for the big, televised singing competition. I rev down the aisle and take the stage, glaring back at Stormy Jackson. This is the journey to my highly anticipated role as Dorothy.

CHAPTER 5

Mr. Reynolds was right. A few seconds later, and it's showtime. If I'm being honest, standing on this stage feels like home. I wring out my hands, sliding them down the crisp pleats on my skirt, as the kids in the audience scoot to the edge of their seats. For about five seconds, I can't hear anything; the world around me is completely muted. By around the ninth second, I start to hear the faint sound of music. It takes a few more beats before I realize it's the intro to my audition song, "Home." I ease the microphone from its stand and wait for my cue. Stormy Jackson sits right below me, in the middle seat, in the first row. The freaky frown on her face could suffocate the song inside me if I let it. I look right past her at the tops of all the heads of the kids in the theater and imagine the *American Rockstar* judges are seated in the back of the theater. Then… I sing.

At first, my voice sounds soft and small, but by the first chorus, I amp up my vocals and hit the crescendo like the composer had me in mind the whole time. Out of the corner of my eye, I spy Mr. Reynolds jotting something onto his clipboard. He sways to the beat of the song while a group of kids in the front row raise their hands and wave them side to side.

"That's my girl!" Georgia yells into the air. "She's fire!"

I close my eyes and sing my heart out, ignoring the daggers Stormy Jackson is pelting into my audition with her eyes. But it doesn't matter; I'm in my zone. Mom and Dad always tell me to connect with my audience, so I take time to walk the stage, making eye contact with the first few rows and singing to them. Twice, I even throw my head back and shake out my big blond curls like there's an imaginary fan blowing in my face. I learned that from studying Queen Beyoncé.

As the song comes to a close, I prep to hit the final note. It's a really big one, too. I suck in all the air around me and release my voice to soar. Then, I take my bow.

"All right, everyone, let's give a round of applause to Lyric Darby."

"Lyric WHITNEY HOUSTON Darby," Twinkie clarifies, as the kids in the middle of the theater snap their fingertips in the air to show they approve.

"Goooooo, Lyric!" a few voices in the crowd yell. I'd bet my fave studded cuff earrings that it's my scout squad.

"Lyr-ic! Lyr-ic!" another voice joins from the front row. When I walk down the steps back to my seat, I can't help but notice the cheerleaders being led in a modified HoneyBee chant by Brooklyn.

"Gimme an *L*!"

"*L*!" the girls yell.

"Gimme a *Y*!"

"*Y*!" they all reply.

"Gimme an *R*!"

"*R*!" I repeat, too.

"Okay, HoneyBees, we get it. I think that's more than enough!" I hear a nasally voice warn from the back of the theater. It's Principal Pootie, wiping his sweaty forehead with his white handkerchief. I don't think there's anyone more devoted to Valentine Middle than him. He appears out of the darkness and barrels down the aisle and onto the stage. We all watch him fidget with his bow tie and stand right in front of Mr. Reynolds. For a few seconds, he scratches his throat before saying, "Let's keep the auditions moving along, thank you very much. I'm sure your support means a lot to Lyric, but we have many other students to get to this afternoon."

Brooklyn and one of her besties, Magic Olive Poindexter, both stand and shoot their thumbs into the air. *I heart them*, I think as I shoot them air thumbs right back.

I slide into my seat beside Georgia and Twinkie, and we have an invite-only giggle fest. We stop only when Mr. Reynolds calls the next person to the stage.

"You were amazy!" Twinkie says as a boy with a green mohawk walks up the stage steps. "I caught it all on my phone. When you watch it back, it might make you cry, though. That's how moving your voice is, Boogie."

Georgia peels Twinkie's fingertips from around the phone. "She legit cried. True story."

"Aw, Twinkie," I gush. "You're always my biggest supporter, my loudest cheerleader."

"Uh, scuse me, but I screamed my head off, too, thank you very much," Georgia says playfully.

"You're the bee's knees. Both of you!"

"It's my job, G," Twinkie explains. "I'm her manager, after all."

"Okay, manager, let's get ready for your—" I'm saying, when Mohawk's voice howls from the stage, causing us all to shriek! He proceeds to take a few very interesting twists and turns through the song before dropping the mic on the floor and walking offstage like he just killed it.

"Okay, let's give Joshua a round of applause," Mr. Reynolds says, but only a few claps and snaps respond.

"Ouch," Twinkie says, looking around at the judgmental crowd of sixth, seventh, and eighth graders. "I hope I don't have to follow that. He totes shifted the mood in here."

She closes her eyes and crosses her fingers, muttering under her breath. "Don't say Saanvi, don't say Saanvi."

"Next up," Mr. Reynolds begins, "is Saanvi Patel."

"Oy!" Georgia peeps. "Sorry, Twink. But it's time to do your thing."

Twinkie glances over at me and shrinks into her seat. "I don't think I can do this."

"You can do anything you put your mind to, dude," Georgia tries to remind her, but it doesn't seem to make a difference because Twinkie slides off her chair and crouches on the floor.

"OMG!" I mutter, mostly to myself, while the rest of the theater looks around for her. "Get up, girl."

"I'll go next," Georgia yells out, standing in the aisle. "Twinkie is, uh, not disposed."

"Indisposed," I correct her.

"Yeah, what she said," Georgia says, walking up to the stage and taking the microphone. "I'm doing this one a capella. It's an original."

"But you're supposed to be singing a song from *The Wiz*. One of the songs the character you want to play sings."

Ignoring Mr. Reynolds, Georgia starts singing her original song before he can even exit stage left.

"What's she doing?" Twinkie asks from under her seat.

"Singing!" I wave at her to stop hiding from the world and rejoin us in her seat. "And she's crushing it," I say, nodding my head to the beat of the cutest, catchiest song I've heard in a while. The rest of the kids agree, if them standing on their feet with their mouths gaping open is any indication. It's clear that she belongs on that stage.

"Thank you, everyone. Rock on!" Georgia says, as she walks offstage, handing the mic to Mr. Reynolds.

"Wow! Wow! Wow!" Twinkie gushes to Georgia when she eases past us to claim her seat. "I soooo wish I could do that."

"You can! You just need to put your mind to it. Focus on what you can do and not what you think you can't."

"It's not that simple," Twinkie says, when Mr. Reynolds moves to the next kid on his list.

Georgia crosses her legs and loosens the top snap on her denim shirt. Then she leans back and pops her suspenders. She knows she's good, and I love that about her. When you have a gift, Jade Darby always says to lean into it; it's what makes you special.

"You're pretty rad, G," I say, and high-five her.

"I do what I can," she says back.

The girl on stage is dressed like the Tin Man and sings "Slide Some Oil to Me" like she just learned it this morning over Froot Loops and turkey bacon. She's meh. If Mr. Reynolds judges Georgia based on her original song, that part belongs to Georgia.

The slew of kids that audition over the next hour is exhausting. I think I might have even rested my eyes for a few of the songs. But when Stormy Jackson takes the stage and does a gorgeous rendition of "Home," I have to admit that I'm a little shook.

"Don't worry, you got this," Georgia says, patting my knee.

My nerves calm when the HoneyBees take the stage and perform the routine they learned before auditions. Brooklyn, Magic, and a few other cheerleaders do their best to crush the cute choreography. I really hope to see them all get cast and prance around that stage in their adorable costumes.

"That was great, dancers," Mr. Reynolds says, clapping his clipboard against his hairy forearm. "I think you'll make fabulous Munchkins."

They really are so stinking cute, I'm thinking, when I turn to Twinkie. As a matter of fact, she'd be cute, too, if I could just convince her to take the stage. Maybe Mr. Reynolds will have better luck. He walks straight over to us.

"Most of the other kids have left, Saanvi. Are you ready to perform your audition now?"

Georgia and I look around the theater. Besides Winnie, our stage manager, there's one student left (and he's the school photographer), so technically, he's still on the clock working.

"What do you think, Twink?" Georgia nudges her. "You can do this. You were born to play the Lion. You'd be so authentic."

"I don't know," she says, standing. "What if I—"

"What?" I ask, pushing her into the aisle. "What if you get the part?"

"Now there's a thought," Georgia says, grabbing her by the hand and leading her to the stage. "I think she's ready, Mr. Reynolds."

Twinkie looks back at me, and I make a heart with my hands. Then I blow her a kiss through the center of it.

That's the last bit of mojo she needs to step onto the stage and take the microphone from the stage manager.

"She's singing for the Lion," Winnie says, wheeling into the wings of the stage.

"Whenever you're ready, Ms. Patel," Mr. Reynolds says, and nods at the pianist, who begins playing "Mean Ole Lion."

Twinkie closes her eyes and steps into the song like she wrote it herself. The photographer snaps several pics of her. Mr. Reynolds nods at Winnie, who hugs herself when Twinkie finishes with more flair than any of the other performers today. Well, most of them.

"That was beautiful," Mr. Reynolds says. "Just beautiful."

Twinkie grins, even though I can still see her hands shaking.

"Saanvi, do you think you'll be able to perform in front of an audience of friends and family when the play opens?"

"Yeah, you'll have to sing in front of real live people," Winnie says. "We won't be able to clear out the theater for your solo."

"I, uh, I mean…"

"She'll be ready, Mr. Reynolds," Georgia says. "I'll make sure of it."

"We'll make sure of it," I add.

Twinkie shrugs, but then she says, "Yes, sir. I'll be ready. I hope."

"I'll keep that in mind as I conference with Winnie and make some big decisions today."

"Thank you, thank you all," Principal Pootie says, shooing us out of the theater. "You all were spectacular, but now it's time to go home. Mr. Reynolds will post the final cast tomorrow. If you make the cut, be prepared for your first rehearsal after school."

"You did it! You were fab!" I tell Twinkie as we leave the Valentine Middle building. We walk our bikes the six blocks to the Promenade for reinforcements at our official headquarters: the Cheesecake Factory.

"I think I have some real competition." Twinkie hoists her backpack over her shoulders. "All those other kids got up there and sang their songs in front of the crowd with no problem."

Georgia picks up a few rocks and tosses them into the bushes. "And? You'll get there."

"We'll help you. And Jade Darby can even give you a few performance tips."

"Yassss!" Twinkie peps. "It doesn't get any better than the one and only Jade Darby of 'Paper Cuts'!"

"I'm sure she'd love to help. The fact that we're doing this musical is her dream come true."

"But what if she finds out about your secret plan?" Georgia asks, chewing on a toothpick.

"If my partners in crime don't tell her, then I'll be in front of the celebrity judges before that ever happens."

Twinkie smushes her face into a question mark. "So, you're seriously not going to tell her?"

"Tell her what?" I shrug, and pop a piece of watermelon bubble gum into my mouth.

I pull the parent consent form from my messenger bag and look at the last line of the official document I downloaded from their website. It reads:

PARENT/GUARDIAN SIGNATURE:

I've never done anything this illegal before. But I made the first move with the audition today. I might as well keep the momentum going.

I take the pen from Georgia.

And I sign her name.

CHAPTER 6

Later that evening, I rush to the dinner table, even though I'm pretty stuffed from cheesecake. I'm a bit pressed because I have a few things I need to run by Mom and Dad. After auditions today, this feels like the best time to shake up the plans for my career around here.

"How were auditions, Boogie?" Mom says as I place my napkin in my lap. "You didn't text me or call. You didn't even post about it on your socials."

Mom puts the final touches on the vegan cheeseburgers and charred (read: burned) broccoli she's making for dinner. I always hope for the best but expect the worst whenever she decides to rock her chef's hat and apron. I've become more of a Grubhub and Uber Eats girl, mainly because my parentals are always on the road and rarely in the kitchen cooking yummy eats for me. When they're gone, Aunt Jackie is their stand-in, and she does her best to keep my belly happy, but she's no Bobby Flay, let me tell you. Auntie's meatloaf and okra definitely don't jam with my culinary palate. Besides, now that I'm a rising star, I have to focus on my long-term health for those intense sessions in the studio that are in my near future.

I watch Mom while simultaneously downloading the Healthy Belly app to my phone. Let's face it, if things go according to plan, it's only a matter of time before I'm opening up for Girl Power. We'll make the perfect concert ticket.

"So, dish the deets, Superstar!" Mom orders as she piles wilted lettuce between the soggy burger buns. I can feel my stomach knotting with each mushy tomato she cuts. I have to do something to save my intestines. I give Dad the stink eye, and he nods in agreement.

"Jade, honey," Dad says sweetly. "Do you think those burgers are a little... wet?"

"What, exactly, are you trying to say, Elvis?" Mom taps her toes into the hardwood floor.

I try sending telepathic messages to Dad's brain,

hoping he stands his ground. He squints at the burgers that Mom is stacking on the island, then he turns back to me. My expression says it all. *PIZZA! PRONTO!*

He doesn't miss a beat. Dad turns away from Mom and hits a few buttons on his phone.

"It's only for emergencies," Dad explains to her when she peeks over his shoulder and huffs loudly into his ear. He reaches for the chips on top of the fridge and dumps them into a ceramic bowl.

"He's right, Mom." I try to cool the sting. Mom has been working on this meal for over an hour. It should only take fifteen minutes to doctor the broccoli and brown the burgers. Seriously, I have no idea what Mom does in the kitchen when no one is around. She doesn't like anyone in her space when she's playing head chef. She always says it's because she needs to concentrate, but Dad and I know better. She doesn't want anyone clowning her technique—if that's what you want to call serving up icky burgers and burned veggies.

"You two do what you want." Mom pouts. "I'll be right here throwing back all this deliciousness."

She brings the platter of disgusting food to the table and sits beside us like she can't see the catastrophe that's right in front of her. She's not one to admit defeat, that's for sure. I kind of like that about her.

"So, Superstar." Dad sits at the table and places the bowl of chips between us. "How'd it go? We've been on pins and needles all day wondering."

I reach for a kale chip and grin. "What do you think?"

"I think you crushed it." He shoves a bunch of chips into his mouth and talks between bites. "You didn't earn the name Superstar because you're great at folding clothes."

"The real question is, were you gracious with the other kids who don't have your big gifts?" Mom asks, trying to keep her messy burger from falling apart. It turns to slop anyway. She takes a big bite, and yep, it slips from her grip, making a mess. On cue, Dad gets up from the table and pads to the fridge, takes out a carton of frozen pad thai, and nukes it for Mom in the microwave. When it's done, he arranges it masterfully on a plate and places it in front of her. I toss the burgers in the trash and grab a set of chopsticks from the junk drawer next to the silverware and hand them to her.

"We love you, honey," Dad says as I massage more unconditional love into her arm.

"Boogie, we're waiting," Mom says, shifting the focus like she always does. We know she's appreciative because she always eats whatever Dad puts in front of her. She just doesn't like to acknowledge it with words. And that's okay with us. Sometimes love can be quiet.

Dad winks at me and I smile. "Okay, folks, if I told you I crushed the audition, would that make you take the next steps that we've been discussing for the past two years?"

"That's my Superstar," Dad says, squeezing my cheeks. "You're going to be big, just give it some time."

"But I'm twelve, Dad, and I'm running out of time."

"But... you're twelve, Boogie." Mom shakes her head. "That's exactly our point. Like you and I discussed at the studio, you're so young. You have the rest of your life to be a sensation."

"We just want you to take the time to enjoy being a healthy, well-adjusted kid for now."

"But the only thing I want to do with my life is sing, Mom."

"And you will. Just give it a little—"

"Time. I know." I sulk. "So does that mean no agent and no manager?"

"For now, Boogie," Mom says, slurping back the slippery noodles. "But in due time, we promise."

"Aw, let the girl sing. If she wants to sing, let her get out there and do her thing," Aunt Jackie says as she heads to bed. "Why all the hoopla about it anyway?"

Dad points to the pizza menu on his phone. "Aren't you going to eat dinner, Auntie?"

"Pizza is not dinner. But that sautéed liver I had tonight…oooh weee!" she pipes, pointing to the broken clock again. "And dinner was three hours ago."

Where do you even find liver in Santa Monica? I wonder, feeling the vomit crawl up my throat. *And who eats dinner at 4:00 PM?*

"Auntie, she's too young to be in the studio and on the road," Mom calls out to Aunt Jackie, who is already heading to her room, her neon-green housecoat blowing in the wind. "We just want you to enjoy being a kid," Mom turns to explain to me.

"But we promise, in due time," Dad says, checking his app for an update on our pizza. "You can take that to the bank."

"But…but…what about the play? What about if I propose something that'll work for all of us?"

"You know we're always down to negotiate," Dad says, putting his phone on the table.

"What about inviting a few agents and managers to opening night of the play? That way, I'm still being a kid, in my kid environment, with my kid musical." I fold my hands on the table. "It's still a win for your favorite kid."

"I don't think so, Boogie," Mom says, finishing the

frozen dinner. She wipes her mouth with a napkin and turns to Dad. "Elvis, tell her what we're thinking."

"Well, Boogie," Dad starts. He rubs his chin and looks away from me when he says, "We're thinking we'll set up a few meetings when you turn eighteen."

"EIGHTEEN!!!" I push my chair from the table and flail my arms in the air like an octopus. "I'll be ancient by then."

I stumble over my chair and storm away from the table.

"Where're you going? Our pizza is turning onto Wilshire." He stands up, too, trying to slow my escape with temptations of gooey cheese and marinara sauce. "Should be here in three minutes."

"I'm never eating pizza again!" I protest, completely lying. He knows it, too. He'll probs drop off a few slices in front of my room, and when he leaves, I'll crack the door and yank the plate inside. In the meantime, I grab an apple from the fruit bowl on the island and bolt up the stairs to my room to drive my point home.

"UGHHH!" I fret behind the closed door of my room, resting my head on the giant poster of Whitney Houston that's been taped to my door since I was four. I check the *American Rockstar* website for the gazillionth time today and close my eyes to pray.

"Dear Whitney Houston, I need you now more than ever. Please help Mom and Dad see the error of their ways. I love you forever. Hugs."

Whitney must've been busy because the next morning was NOT the vibe. I woke up to my very own note from Mom that sent my mental fitness down a dark, winding road.

Dear Boogie, Dad and I had to leave early this morning for a last-minute gig in Reno. We'll be gone for a few weeks, but when we get back, we promise to pick up our conversation where we left off. We know how important your singing career is to you.

We love you very much. Wish us luck. xo

P.S. Aunt Jackie will be right down the hall.

I sit with the note in my hands, gripping it for dear life. After a few seconds, I notice that the ink in the center of the notebook paper is blotched. That's when I realize that maybe a few tears have fallen and settled into Mom's empty promises about not leaving me again. I can't seem to wrap my brain around why she doesn't want to be here for my so-called life. She's choosing to be in Reno instead of here with me. Reno! It isn't even Vegas! Why can't I be enough? At least more important than... Reno!

I try to shower, but I end up sitting on the edge of the tub, dry heaving. I hate when the feelings of hopelessness start to creep in. I always end up overwhelmed with sadness. And I don't really have an appetite, not even a craving for pizza from Fat Sal's. It's all so weird and confusing.

My head hangs and the cold water drips from the ends of my curls onto my knees. I sob, thinking about all the racing thoughts telling me that I'm not good enough—or even worse, that I'm not worthy of Mom's love. I know that's not true, but I can't get that tape that's on rewind in my mind to shut off.

I ball my fist and slam it down onto the side of the tub.

I wish I could make it all just go away. I've been dealing with this kind of stinkin' thinkin' for a few years. I call them my mental monsters, and they seem to show up whenever Mom leaves.

I grip the ends of my hair and squeeze, reminding myself that no one can know about my private brain pain. It has to stay that way. It's not like I can tell Mom; I'd never want to burden her while she's on the road working. But TBH, I don't know what to do about it. All I do know is this is the exact reason why I have to blow up and become a star. If my name is in lights, she'll have to see me then. Maybe then the brain pain will go away.

But until that day comes, I do what I always do.

I stand in front of the bathroom mirror and say to the girl with the red, puffy eyes, "You are a star. Pull it together. You're Jade Darby's daughter. A star."

That's when I hear a ding on my phone, and I know exactly who it is.

> Twinkie: 2day the cast is being posted. U ready, superstar?

If I get cast as Dorothy, I'll be one step closer to getting and keeping Mom's attention. So I take more minutes than I should to pull myself together. Then I shove my feelings deep down inside and cover them up with fabulousness and concealer. Today, I'm feeling disconnected from it all. So it's a fringes kind of day.

When I get to school, I'm a frazzled mess. Before I read Mom's note, I'd barely slept. It was Twinkie's fault. She has this insomniac thing. She loves to group text in the middle of the night, and when it's something important, I get roped into the thread. But they have to be important musings, because believe me, when I'm not stuck in my looping thoughts when Mom is gone, I'm always the junior ambassador for beauty sleep.

"Did they post the cast yet?!" Georgia asks as I take a deep breath and remember to smile over the leftover frown. I open my locker before turning to her.

She gasps.

"What?! I don't look *that* bad." I check the garbage bags under my eyeballs in my locker mirror. "I mean... do I?"

"No, you're gorge, as always," Twinkie affirms, poking Georgia in the ribs. But Georgia's smirk says the complete opposite.

"Whatevs. It's not like I could get any sleep with Twinkie texting us into the wee hours of the night."

"I was freaking out. I still am! What if I don't get cast?!" She opens her locker, and her entire head disappears inside again. Georgia and I wait for her to fish out her stuff. She grabs her textbooks and lip gloss before her head pops out to gripe, "Or worse. What if I *do* get cast?"

"Everything's going to work out," I insist. "It just has to. There's a bigger plan in place here. Okay, so follow my thoughts. First, the cast will be posted today, then play rehearsals start after school, and then again tomorrow morning, and thennnnnn... *American Rockstar* auditions next week. I'll def be ready cuz I will have had a whole week working on my signature song with Ms. Pepper." I twirl my curl around my finger. "What could possibly go wrong?"

"You make it sound so easy," Twinkie says, with a hint of doubt in her voice. We can't have doubt infiltrating our theater squad. Fact: If there was ever a weak link in a secret operation, it would be Twinkie. You know, the one who flails, who bungles the whole thing, but doesn't mean to.

"It *is* easy," I reassure her. "As long as everything goes according to plan."

"Don't think for a split second that you're the voice of Valentine Middle," Stormy Jackson says, barreling up to me, waving her arms over her head.

"Whoa, whoa, whoa!" Georgia steps in front of her, shielding me from her gross spit.

"What's your deal, Stormy?" I ask.

Her purple-and-white sequined vest is blinding. I cover my eyes when she yells, "I may be your understudy, but all I need is for you to have one slipup and that role is MINE! MINE!"

We watch her awkwardly standing there, snarling and staring at me for what feels like an eternity. Then she just turns and stomps down the hallway yelling to anyone who passes, "I'm a Jackson. A Jackson!"

"What was she even talking about?" Twinkie asks, but Georgia and I have already put the puzzle pieces together.

I grab Twinkie by the sleeve of her Valentine Middle gym tee and beeline down the hall behind Georgia, who's motoring toward the theater.

"OMG! OMG!" Georgia geeks as her fingers scroll down the cast list that's taped to the bulletin board outside the theater.

"Did she make it?" Twinkie stands on her tiptoes to see over Georgia's jean jacket. The tassels hanging from Georgia's shoulder smack Twinkie in the face. "Did she?"

Georgia swings around to look at us and smiles at Twinkie. "And so did you!"

"It just got real," Twinkie says, her face flushing as she presses the back of her hand over her forehead.

"You'll be a smash," Georgia says to her. "Just keep being our little drama queen that we love."

Then they both look at me as I step up to the roster and read the first few cast members' names to myself.

THE WIZ
FINAL CAST
DOROTHY: Lyric Darby
SCARECROW: Georgia Reign
LION: Saanvi Patel

TIN MAN: Buster Wallace

MUNCHKINS: The HoneyBee Dancers

"So, Dorothy?" Twinkie asks, her eyes beaming. "Looks like step one of the master plan is complete."

Georgia puts her hand on my shoulder and smiles deviously. "*American Rockstar,* you're up next."

I think of what it all means. *American Rockstar,* then . . . Mom. "I'm finally getting closer."

Twinkie grabs my hand and squeezes it tightly. "How's it all feel?"

I stare at my name on the roster and envision myself at the big audition in eight days! "Well, Twinkie, I don't think we're in Kansas anymore."

CHAPTER 7

Saturday.

7:56 AM.

"This is the beginning of something magical," Georgia says as we sit on the steps of the school, waiting for Mr. Reynolds to arrive and open the doors to Valentine Middle. I'm never at school on the weekends for any of the extracurriculars, so it feels weird to be here on my day off, because, yeah, twelve-year-olds need days off, too.

"I think I'm biting off more than I can swallow," Twinkie says.

"Chew," Georgia says, matter-of-fact.

"But I don't have anything in my mouth," she answers back.

"No. That's not how the saying goes." Georgia makes air quotes to drive her point home. "It's 'biting off more than you can chew,' not 'swallow.'"

"Oh. Well, whatevs." Twinkie shrugs. "You get my point about this. How did I get here? It was only supposed to be fun for auditions. Like a singing exercise." She slouches into herself and whines, "Yesterday's rehearsal was just passing out the scripts and doing a few ice breakers. But today . . . today is the day where—"

"It's about to go DOWN!" Georgia finishes with all the flair.

"You're going to be an amazing talent up there on that stage," I tell Twinkie. I mean it, too. "You're the real deal. Now it's time for everyone to discover what we've known forever."

A few more kids get dropped off in front of the school before Mr. Reynolds races around the corner and up the stairs to unlock the building. He's frazzled but calms when all the kids start applauding for him. It's obvi he's not just my fave teacher.

"Okay, everyone, welcome to the first full day of rehearsals for our spring musical, *The Wiz*!" Mr. Reynolds says, hopping onto the stage. Winnie rolls her wheelchair backstage to turn on all the lights in the house while Lucy unlocks the walk-in wardrobe closet.

"I'm excited to see all of you," he says as Magic and Brooklyn walk in together, with two football players, Dallas Chase and Logan Smith, behind them.

"This is going to be iconic!" Georgia yells at the stage.

"We love that enthusiasm, Georgia," Mr. Reynolds says. "This is your production, so I want you all to give it one hundred ten percent of your love, talent, and attention. Now that we've all had a day to get to know each other and highlight our scripts, today we'll begin rehearsing."

He goes on about how special every role is in the play and explains that there are no small parts, only small actors.

"Yeah, that's true, cuz I'm pretty small," Twinkie says, missing the point. But she's right; besides our cheer team's newest flyer, LuLu, Twinkie is the tiniest kid in the play.

"That's not what he means," Georgia starts explaining, but then she just shrugs and pats Twinkie on the shoulder. She shifts gears, proud of herself, but not in a braggy way. "I learned mostly everyone's part. I couldn't really sleep last night, so I pulled up the play and got into it."

"That's bananas," I say back to her, my eyes saucering at the thought. "Like all of the big parts?"

"I mean, yeah," Georgia says, like it's totally normal to

memorize most of a play in a night. “Evilene is my fave. I just heart a mean old witch.”

“I hope you learned my part, too, because I’m not so sure I can do this,” Twinkie says as we all move to the front of the stage to do the first official read-through of the play.

I tap my finger on my chin and lean closer to whisper-announce, “I’m thinking of having a watch party at my house.”

“Which version are you showing?” Georgia asks.

“We can vote. I’m a modern girl, so I’m into the one with Queen Latifah and Amber Riley.”

“I love Amber Riley,” Twinkie says, ear-hustling.

“But the original is so much better,” Stormy says, poking her pigtailed head into our private conversation. “Because of—”

“Michael Jackson,” me and Georgia say in unison, rolling our eyes.

Stormy snarls at us and coughs up a big “Duh!”

“But no one was talking to you,” Georgia snaps.

“I’m still invited, right? I mean, I am part of this production.”

“Of course you are, Stormy,” I offer, taking a copy of the play from one of the heavy stacks that’s being passed around to everyone.

Georgia pinches her lips and cuts her eyes. "Fine. Just don't bring over any of his memorabilia. Leave that at home. Puh-lease."

Stormy turns back around in her seat proudly. "I'll bring popcorn. And...thank you."

"Why did you do that?" Georgia whispers, pinching me.

"Because she's part of the cast." I pat Georgia's knee and reassure her. "We're all in this together. It'll be fine."

But Georgia isn't done ranting. "If she plays one video from the *Thriller* album, I'm out."

"All right, thespians," Mr. Reynolds says, sitting criss-cross applesauce in the middle of the stage. "Let's do a quick run-through and then divide into groups to rehearse." He glances over the first two rows of actors until he spots Stormy. "And, Stormy, you're not just the understudy for Dorothy; I want you to learn all the parts, or as many as you can. You'll be the floating understudy."

"What about me?" Georgia pipes.

"You're playing the Scarecrow, Georgia."

"I know that, Mr. R, but it's just that I learned all the parts last night."

"You what?" he asks, the corners of his mouth turning up into a smile. "All the parts?"

"I mean...yeah. So if you need me to—"

"That's amazing. I'll keep that in mind in case of emergency," he reassures her. Then he circles back and says like a proud papa, "Wow."

That's Georgia for you. She's disorganized and usually scattered. But when she's invested in something that makes her heart dance, the girl is on fire. Even though I don't understand how she does it, I love that about her.

"Let's take it from the top," Mr. Reynolds says.

We read through the script twice. Mr. Reynolds stops us to give notes and explain parts of the story that some kids don't understand. He takes the time to answer questions and encourage each of us. To be honest, I'm actually enjoying this. By the time we're done with the second read-through, I'm excited to practice a few songs and start blocking. Before I know it, it's time to get fitted for my costume. I don't allow myself to get too caught up. I know I have to crush my competition next Saturday and shine for the judges, and no matter what I do, I can't let the musical become a distraction.

CHAPTER 8

***Today should be named National* American Rockstar** Day.

It's the only day that matters in my world. An entire week passed, and it's like it never happened. I gave up on focusing on Monday. By Wednesday, I was sitting through all my classes, twiddling my thumbs, checking out all the *American Rockstar* auditions from past seasons online. Mr. Chang almost busted me a few times, but Twinkie did this thing to get my attention. It worked, but at what cost? It sounded like a frog was choking her esophagus. Now I feel bad for her poor throat. I'm sorry, but *American*

Rockstar was my newest obsession, and Chang's number puzzles just couldn't compete. Neither could the musical and Mr. Reynolds.

Getting through four hours of rehearsal today was brutal. All I could think about was getting my squad in tow so we could scramble down to the Pier and snag my spot in line. *American Rockstar* is only allowing a certain number of people to audition, and once they're all in line, that's it. No more. Done. Finito. And I get it, they don't want to be at the Pier until midnight listening to a bunch of non-famous folks singing some popular Adele song. I would've bribed my scout squad, or even Magic, to hold my place for *American Rockstar,* but they're all in the play, too. Thank goodness the Pier is only a ten-minute bike ride from school. Just a few blocks to Wilshire, then a few more streetlights to Ocean Avenue—and it's smooth sailing from there. I don't have a second to waste; it's time to make moves that are sure to change my life forever.

I'm at the intersection of Ocean Avenue and Colorado, checking out the line for auditions. It's zigzagging around the entire block. Twice! And while the traffic on Ocean is usually bumper-to-bumper, today it's a parking lot.

"How are we ever going to get to the front of this line?" Twinkie asks, standing on her tippy-toes to get a glimpse of all the hopefuls here for their big shot at stardom. "By the time we get up there to get our numbers, get signed in and in front of the judges, it'll be tomorrow."

"Says who?" Georgia asks, kicking the tire on her red-and-white dirt bike. "You gotta stay positive. Let's just get to the back of the line and save our spots."

Twinkie hops off her bike and stomps her little feet into the pavement. "Are you seeing what I'm seeing? That line is all the way up the Pier, past Bubba Gump Shrimp, the arcade, the Lobster, and way back to Second Street by the McDonald's."

But Georgia is already pedaling toward the McDonald's, waving at all the kids and some of the adults in line. "C'mon! With all these peeps, I bet it's only a matter of time before they shut the line down."

We race to the back of the line, and when we turn the corner, we bump into a guy with a walkie-talkie proudly wearing a black tee and a neon-yellow windbreaker that says PRODUCER over his heart. He looks pretty cool and official in his outfit, but I don't like the fact that he's blocking the line.

"Hi, uh...," I say, trying to catch my breath. "I'm, uh... here to—"

We lock our bikes at the bike stand in front of the McDonald's. Georgia moves in front of me and tries to explain. "She's here to audition. Soooo can you move over so she can stand behind the man with the flood pants and thick socks?"

I gasp when the producer denies me entry to my dream, saying in slow motion, "Girls, this is the cutoff for auditions today. We are at capacity."

"What does that even mean?" I ask.

"You'll have to come back next year."

Twinkie scans my body with her hands. "Do you even know who she is?" When he doesn't answer with the resounding *YES* she's expecting, Twinkie continues. "She's—"

"I don't care. She could be the best singer in the universe, and it wouldn't matter. Those are the rules. The line closed ten minutes ago."

"OMG! What am I going to do now?" I cry out, walking away while Georgia flashes him her best "cutest girl in the world" smile. That ship has sailed, though. And he doesn't budge.

"What are we going to do now?" Twinkie asks me, sitting on the curb at the end of the block.

"I want a double cheeseburger," Georgia says, watching a little girl with a head full of pigtails walk out of the McDonald's with a Happy Meal. "It'll help me think."

"We have to come back next year. That line is barely

moving, and neither is that security producer guy," Twinkie says. "I can't think of any other way."

"There's always a way," I say, trying to remain in control and focused on building a new master plan.

I lead them back down the two blocks to Ocean Avenue and scope out all the mazes of ropes and blocked-off sidewalks that are keeping people confined in the organized chaos. "Wow. This is a whole thing."

We walk past all the people in line warming up their voices or practicing their songs. I finally stop to sit on one of the benches beside the entrance to the Pier. I just need a few seconds to rest my feet and think.

"Yeah. This is way more intense than I thought it would be," Twinkie says, retrieving her stickered thermos from her backpack.

"You shouldn't drink that. You know you have the world's smallest bladder," I say, glancing at the Porta Potties. "I mean... unless..."

"Good point," Twinkie says, but she takes a few big gulps anyway before shoving the thermos back into her bag.

"So... what's the plan?" Georgia asks me as I stand up to sneak a peek at the madness happening just beyond the overlook. Everything looks super Hollywood. I spy camera crews, producers running around, and long trailers parked beside one another. The sand and ocean are in the distance behind it all, creating the perfect Southern California backdrop. I sigh, longing to be part of the madness now even more than before.

"What's happening down there?" Twinkie asks, sneaking a long sip of her water.

"At least ten tents next to the Pier in the oversize parking lot." I crane my neck to see around the giant man in front of me with his toddler hoisted over his shoulders. "I guess that's where they're doing the prelims."

"Do you see any blind spots?" Twinkie asks, taking another big gulp.

Georgia laces her shoes, twisting her head to declare, "We should be able to slip in somewhere. We know this pier better than anyone."

Twinkie stands and starts a slow dance. She moves from side to side, tapping her feet on the cement. I roll my eyes when she grabs her belly. I'd know that dance anywhere.

"You better not say you have to pee," Georgia scoffs, but Twinkie's smile turns upside down, and her secret isn't really a secret at all.

"Seriously, Twink? Can you hold it?" Georgia's cheeks turn red like they always do whenever she's annoyed.

"She's fine," I say, turning to Twinkie. "You're fine, right?"

Twinkie shakes her head *NO*, but then she says, "I can hold it. I think."

I squeeze her hand and pull her down the long ramp that leads to Bubba Gump Shrimp. "Good. Cuz we have to find the back way into this circus so we can skip the line. Tell your bladder that now is not the time."

The crowd is already restless, and honestly, I don't blame them. That's when I overhear a girl, dressed like a hipster, gripping a guitar case. My heart sinks when she says she's been in line since three o'clock this morning.

"We def can't cut anyone," I whisper to Georgia. "They'll murder us."

My dreams are deflating right in front of Bubba Gump Shrimp.

I check and discover that every single opening to the parking lot is blocked. There's only one way in and one way out of the tent village the TV show has set up for contestants. *Ugh!*

"Lyric, I'm so sorry," Twinkie whines. "But I really *really*—"

"I knew it," Georgia scoffs. "Your bladder is like clockwork. One sip of water and you open up like a waterfall."

"I really REALLY gotta go."

"We can try Bubba Gump," I say, but when we get to the front door, the sign on the door practically yells at us.

RESTROOMS ARE NOT FOR *AMERICAN ROCKSTAR* CONTESTANTS...LYRIC!

Or at least that's what it might as well have said!

"Let's just find you a Porta Potti," I grumpy-utter, accepting the fact that I won't be hitting that mega stage this year.

"No. I hate those things. They're gross. And they're..." Twinkie stops talking and starts fast-dancing, bouncing up and down with her feet crossed at the ankles. "I need a real bathroom."

"Okey doke," I say.

She looks around at the zillions of people populating the Pier. "You two keep looking for a back way to get in line. I'll find a place." She can barely see over any of their heads. "Somewhere. Out there."

I put my arm over her shoulder and pull her closer to my heart. "No, that's not how we roll. We stick together."

"I'm so sorry, Lyric. I know you've been dreaming of this day since second grade in Ms. Cornfoot's class. The first time you saw this TV show at Georgia's seventh birthday party, you couldn't take your eyes off the TV screen. You almost passed out in a bowl of Flamin' Hot Cheetos."

"There's always next year," I offer, holding back tears. "The only thing I know how to do is sing, so that's just what I'll do." I sigh. "Next year."

"Lyric," Twinkie whisper-cries. "I can't hold it anymore."

I shake off the overwhelming feeling of defeat and focus on Twinkie's pee. "Let's try Hot Dog on a Stick. They might let you use their bathroom. Stella Rose's brother, Arlo, works there."

By the time Twinkie wobbles over to the historic hot dog cart, she can barely speak. She stands on the balls of her feet and says to the girl with the pointy nose wearing the black hairnet, "Can . . . Me . . . Bathroom . . ."

I push past a few people in line until I spy the ca-yootest guy.

"Arlo. Arlo! Remember me?" I gush. "I'm Stella Rose's friend. From her scout troop. We're Sunflowers together."

"Oh. Okay," he says, putting a bunch of wooden sticks in piles next to the grill. "What's up?"

I point to Twinkie, and my eyebrows dip into my forehead. Everyone around us in line can see that, at this point, it's a do-or-pee emergency. Arlo wastes no time ushering her back to the bathroom, and by the time she disappears behind the hot dog stand, she's almost in tears. Georgia and I wait next to the ketchup and mustard in front of the sliding window. When I feel a single tear sliding down my cheek, I shake it off and do that one thing I know how to do.

I sing.

At first, it's mainly me singing to my shoestrings.

♪♪ *When I think of home, I think of a place*
Where there's love overflowing...

But then I sing some more, mostly to the ketchup bottle.

And then I sing louder, this time to the plastic utensils beside the condiments.

And harder, focusing for the first time on the small crowd that's surrounding me.

And then the crowd grows bigger, so I sing my heart out until I'm starting to feel much better. I throw my hands into the air, fling my head back, and swing my curls in the air as I hold my notes like my twelve-year-old life depends on it. I open my eyes when I hear a curious voice in the distance.

"Excuse me," I hear a woman's voice say as she pushes through the crowd. "Excuse me."

"Hey," I answer her, stopping before the next verse. I check her out, balancing three hot dogs on a stick with a cup of french fries and funnel cake sticks. She glances around at the crowd that's now clapping and whistling for me.

"Are you by any chance auditioning today?"

"No. I mean... yeah. I mean, that was the plan but not now."

There's a glimmer that I spy in her eyes when she asks, "Why not?"

"Did you see that monster of a line? That sucker is wrapped all the way back to Second Street in front of the bicycle shop." I shrug. "So, by the time I get to the judges, it'll be midnight. Not to mention that the Incredible Hulk producer wouldn't even let me *get* on the line."

She lowers her voice and looks around suspiciously. "How old are you?"

"Twelve. And a half." I fold my arms over my chest. "Why?"

"What if I told you I'm one of the judges? Well, I'm actually a junior producer, and we're judging the first few rounds of auditions before contestants move on. You know, to the celebrity judges."

If I wasn't leaning against the food cart, I think my knees would've buckled and I would've fallen face-first right into her snacks.

Georgia shoves me closer to the producer, and I almost kiss her nose.

She whisper-asks, "Do you by any chance have industry experience?"

Before I can answer, Georgia whips her hair around and beams. "She's playing the lead role in *The Wiz.*"

"She's the one and only Lyric Whitney Houston Darby," Twinkie adds, rushing up to us, still wringing out her wet hands. "This budding superstar beat out the whole school for the role of Dorothy—even Michael Jackson's second niece, twice removed—on his mother's side."

The woman looks down at her denim overalls and black tee and cracks a smile. "I see."

Twinkie rocks back and forth on her yellow Vans sneakers and professes to the whole crowd, "It's going to be the biggest musical of the year in all of Santa Monica. Some of the drama kids from Valentine High are even coming."

"Well. Look at that," the woman says. "It's really nice to meet you, Lyric Whitney Houston Darby." She surveys all the snacks in her arms. When she can't shake my hand, she just nods. "I'm Bailey. Your new best friend. I think you have exactly what we're looking for. I haven't heard a voice like yours since we started this thing this year." She steps back and surveys my vibe. "How's your social media following?"

"I have a few thousand followers," I boast proudly, but when she winces, I second-guess my bragging.

"You think you could get that up to at least ten thousand? Maybe even twenty, or what about fifty? That would really make a difference, since we're quietly looking for contestants with big Insta followings. We do make exceptions from time to time, but it's sort of an unwritten rule and would guarantee you a spot down the line for the live taping with the final sixty-four, should you make it that far."

I try to keep my cool, but this is huge—and it's all happening right here in front of Hot Dog on a Stick.

"Of course she can," Twinkie says, waving off that gargantuan request. I smile along with Georgia, whose eyes are darting around the crowd. Whenever she does this, I know she's doing the math in her head, only this time, there's no need. No arrangement of numbers is going to equal me getting TEN THOUSAND FOLLOWERS!!

She motions for Twinkie to dig in her back pocket. I watch Twinkie's tiny fingers disappear into Bailey's denim. And then it happens. Twinkie pulls out an oversize laminated platinum ticket that reads in big bold letters:

AMERICAN ROCKSTAR
ROUND 2

"Ohmahgawd!!!" all three of us shriek.

I try stringing words together to make sense of it all. "Is that... like... is that what—what I think it is?"

"Lyric Whitney Houston Darby, would you like to come back in two weeks for the second round of auditions for *American Rockstar*?"

I mouth the word *YES*! But nothing comes out of my mouth.

"There will be tons of good singers by then, and we'll start digging deeper, you know, vetting you even more at that point." She shrugs and smiles. "But if everything pans out, I don't see any reason why you can't go really far in this competition."

"Thank you. You won't regret it," I say, rocking back and forth on my tiptoes.

She waves and leaves with her armful of snacks. I wave back and exhale victory because thanks to Twinkie's bladder, I'm back in the game.

CHAPTER 9

"How am I ever going to get fifty thousand or even twenty thousand followers?!" I rant as we walk into Mr. Chang's math class Monday morning, still trying to process the baby Jesus miracle that went down two days ago at Hot Dog on a Stick. I wipe the sweat beads from my left temple. "And I'm expected to do that in two weeks?!"

"She said ten thousand first. Let's shoot for that," Twinkie says, skipping into the room.

"We'll do all the textbook stuff," Georgia suggests, shoving a toothpick between her teeth. "Like... we'll play to all your strengths."

"Yeah, and you have a ton," Twinkie says, sliding into the desk beside me. "You can sing. You can dance. You can act."

Georgia points her toothpick at me and winks. "A total triple threat."

"Yeah, that's all true," I say, tapping my chin for more mojo. "Let's make a list of all the popular songs I should cover." I take a long sip of my venti frothed coffee and think deeply. "I need to get started right after school. We have less than two weeks before I'm in front of the TV producers again."

"So, what's the plan?" Twinkie asks.

Georgia jams her overstuffed backpack under her desk. "I think your mom is one of your biggest strengths. She could really help you boost your following."

"G's right," Twinkie agrees. "She endorsed Brooklyn for the big Valentine Middle cookie contest, and that put her over the top." Then she thinks. "Well, almost."

Georgia plops into the seat and shrugs. "She still lost, but it helped."

"Dudes! My mom can't know anything about this. Nothing. Nada." I shush them both, even though neither of them is talking.

"You really don't think she'd support you trying to get cast on the show?" Twinkie asks, squinting her eyes like she's trying to see into the future. "You already made it this far. I bet only about half of that whole line of peeps advanced to the second round."

"No. She'd shut it all down. Jade Darby can't know anything about *American Rockstar*. Are we clear? Like crystal clear?"

They both nod and pinky swear to keep my secret, just as the bell rings and Mr. Chang finishes writing the last math problem on the board. When he moves out of the way, I see the two words every kid hates!

POP QUIZ

"You gotta be kidding!" Georgia throws her hands into the air.

Mr. Chang turns to her and glares, never saying a word. She takes the hint and shuts her trap.

"Ten minutes, class," Mr. Chang says as everyone pulls out paper and begins solving the problem.

I can see Georgia's attention drift into a universe that has nothing to do with probability. She stares out the window for the first few minutes before finally turning to focus on her blank paper. Then she scribbles tons of... words. Not numbers!

What are you doing? I mouth the words at her.

"Your set list," she whisper-answers, a little too loud.

Before I can warn her, Mr. Chang walks right down our aisle and stops when he gets to our desks.

NO!

"It's a pop quiz, Ms. Darby and Ms. Reign. That means no talking."

"Sorry," I say, trying to get him to focus on my desk and not Georgia's. But it doesn't work.

"What are you doing over here, Ms. Reign? None of this looks like math."

He takes the paper from Georgia and begins reading aloud. "'Ariana Grande. Princess Taylor Swift. Queen Beyoncé. Selena Gomez. The one and only Queen Beyoncé again.'"

Georgia snatches the paper from him and tries to explain, "It's a set list and it's very important."

"Do you not understand that your pop quiz is the only thing you should be focused on right now? Have I not made that clear?"

"But, Mr. Chang, someone's life LITERALLY depends on that list of icons right now."

"No. Your life depends on this quiz." He bends down to face Georgia until they are eye to eye. "You're failing my math class, Ms. Reign."

"But. Dude."

"I'll just hold on to this and show it to your parents tomorrow morning at our parent-teacher conference. I think it's a good example of where your head is, because it isn't in my math class. Dude."

"But they'll take me out of the play, Mr. Chang."

"You should've thought of that before you decided to get into the music biz and become someone's manager."

"Actually, sir, I'm the manager," Twinkie peeps, claiming her job.

"Do you really want to be part of this, Ms. Patel?" he asks as Twinkie immediately shifts her focus back to her quiz.

Mr. Chang stands up straight, still holding the paper in his hands. "Ms. Reign?"

"Let me guess. Detention. Again."

Later that afternoon, Twinkie and I hang outside Mr. Chang's room, waiting for Georgia to be released from after-school jail. We're in a heated debate about who is the best artist for me to cover. She's convinced that tagging them will get their attention, and the followers will, well, follow.

"There's no way Ariana Grande won't get everyone's eyes on you," Twinkie says, pointing her phone at my face to show me Ariana's page. "I bet you a Pinkberry swirl that we get at least one hundred new followers from tagging her in a post of you covering one of her hits."

"I'm into it. Let's see what happens," I say, now standing in front of the big palm tree on the school's perfectly landscaped lawn. I clear my throat and pull up the instrumental version of "Thank U, Next."

"Ready?" Twinkie says, getting a close-up of my face. I shut my eyes and channel my inner superstar just like Jade Darby, flashing my chin dimple.

"Born ready!" I say as she cues the music.

I start the song and Twinkie circles me, panning the camera phone around the tree as I throw my head back and shake out my curls. I look into the camera and give it my award-winning smize. *It's all happening*, I think to myself as I finish the song with a singular, velvety note.

"That was très fierce," Twinkie peps, uploading the video onto my IG: @xo_lyric. "Now, we need to tag a few key legends in the game and hit a few more hot spots around town."

"What do you have in mind, manager?"

"I'm thinking we cruise to the beach. That'll be a cool backdrop for your songs." She shows me the footage she just captured and smiles to herself. "Pretty good, huh?"

"Yeah. It is, actually. Maybe you do have a management agency in your future, after all."

"Duh," she answers back. "And it helps to have you as the muse. Plus, you're a one-take wonder. My little cousins make me record them at least twenty times before we can even think about posting to TikTok."

"Let's do another one," I suggest, getting excited about what's to come. At the rate we're going, we should be able to record all the dopest chart-toppers that fit my voice and get some serious followers. "We only have this week and next week to make a dent, Twink."

"You already have two thousand seventy-six followers," she says, scrolling through my Insta. "That's a good start."

I roll my eyes, not keeping that same energy as Twinkie. "That's *nawt* a good start, Twink."

"Well, with some Queen B, we should def be able to amp up the love on your page."

Maybe she's right, I think, trying to stay anchored in the positive. I flip through my phone until I find the perfect Beyoncé song to cover.

"Cute, huh?" Twinkie says as she shoots me singing like we're filming a music video.

"More like H-O-T," Georgia says, barreling out of the school building.

"You're running like the place is on fire," I clown Georgia. "They let you out of jail, or did you escape?"

"I served my time," she says. "Let's get out of here before the warden changes his mind though."

"You got it, sister!" Twinkie says, grabbing her backpack and passing her phone to Georgia. "Check out what we did while you were behind bars."

"This is legit sick," Georgia says. "You already look like a star!"

"Because she is," Twinkie gushes. "She's my first client at my management agency, and now we have to get our star to the ocean for sunset. The golden hour will be the perfect backdrop for her next song."

I lean into Georgia, admiring the magic Twinkie helped make happen. "The golden hour is definitely my thing. The sun against this melanin is très magnificent."

We head to the beach and splash around the shoreline for another hour or so, recording song after song. Georgia gave me her jacket, and Twinkie shoved my hair into an updo for different looks. Then we tagged and hashtagged our hearts out, making sure to include the artists and some of their most engaged followers.

"Do you think we should tag *American Rockstar*?" Twinkie asks as we walk across the bridge back to Ocean Avenue after sunset. "They need to know how lucky they are that you want to team up with them."

"Brillz idea," I agree. "I think it'll be a sick partnership. They only have millions of viewers, and every winner they've chosen gets to tour all around the world. So"—I tap my chin and grin—"I think it'll be a mutually beneficial relationship."

"You're thinking like a big brand," Georgia says, motioning for Twinkie to take our picture. "Get in, too, Twinkie. Let's snap a pic to always remember this moment in time."

I push Georgia away and say, "No. Just me, Twink." I pose for a few fake candid shots, staring longingly into the sunset. "I *am* the moment."

Georgia immediately wraps her palm around the camera phone and spouts back, "Looks more like you're a twelve-year-old diva-in-the-making. Stop that right now." She wriggles her finger in the air at me. "It's not always about you. It can be about us sometimes, too."

"Yeah, Boogie," Twinkie says, curling her upper lip like she smells something stinky. "Nobody likes *that* girl."

I shrug it off like it's no big deal even though the picture would've been glorious. Whatevs. There'll be plenty of time for red carpet photos taken by celeb photographers where I'm headed.

Georgia waits for me to smile, signaling to her that she's right. I open my arms for G to scoot closer for a squad pic, and she happily joins. "That's more like it." She gestures for Twinkie to squeeze in, too. "Much better," she hypes as Twinkie ussies us to death. "We're all in this together."

When we're done with our mini photo shoot, Georgia hops on her bike and turns down the street, saluting us with a "Later, gators."

"Hey, G," I say before she's out of earshot. "Don't worry about the thingy with Chang and your peeps tomorrow. It'll be okay."

"Yeah, and if it isn't, we'll get Mr. Reynolds involved," Twinkie says, snapping her fingers. "He always has your back."

"I guess." Georgia forces a smile. "It is what it is."

Georgia was always good for leaving things in the hands of the universe. Me, not so much. I'd already decided to talk to Mr. Reynolds first thing in the morning. I can't risk letting my girl get kicked out of the play. It's one of the few things she really loves, and she's good at it, too. I just wish adults understood that sometimes we need what we need to be happy. And for all three of us, it happens to be one singular place on the planet.

The stage.

CHAPTER 10

"Mr. Reynolds! Mr. Reynolds!" I yell as he crosses the street, heading for school. I'd been sitting outside the building for twenty minutes waiting for him to arrive. I figured that if I could get to him before the morning rush, I'd have a better chance of advocating for Georgia's life as a thespian.

"Good morning to you, too, Lyric. Or should I say… Dorothy?"

"No time for witty banter right now," I rattle, shaking my venti caramel macchiato. "It's life or death. Like, a serious ten on the being-twelve-meter."

"What's the haps?" he asks, opening the front door and holding it for me. "I have about five minutes before I'm swarmed with school stuff."

"It's Georgia!"

"What's wrong with our Scarecrow?"

"That's just it. If you don't step in, we'll be Scarecrow-less, Mr. Reynolds."

"Is it Mr. Chang again?"

I nod and usher him toward Mr. Chang's class, explaining everything he needs to know about the parent conference and her failing grades.

"I knew she was struggling, but not this much," he says, knocking on Mr. Chang's door.

"Come in, Mr. Reynolds," Mr. Chang says when he looks up from his desk.

I glance around the room and see Georgia and her parents sitting in front of Mr. Chang's desk. He's holding her pop quiz from yesterday that doubled as my set list. Now, I'm not a detective, but the look on her father's face told me everything I needed to know, and let's just say it was a good thing that I waited outside today for reinforcements.

Mr. Chang passes the smoking gun to Georgia's mother and says, "This was her pop quiz from yesterday." Then he turns to us and says, "What can I do for you, Mr. Reynolds? We're in the middle of a meeting." He shakes his head into an annoyed *tsk*. "And, Ms. Darby, this is a closed meeting."

"Please let them stay," Georgia begs. "They're the only ones who really seem to get it."

When Mr. Chang throws his hands into the air, Mr. Reynolds takes that as his cue and wastes no time pulling up a chair. I follow his lead. But before he can say anything, I insert myself into the convo. It's just that Georgia looks like she's about to explode and cry all over her country western outfit.

"Please, Mr. and Mrs. Reign, forgive the interruption," Mr. Reynolds begins. Then I interrupt him.

"Yes, not to intrude," I start, even though I would've shut the whole meeting down to save my girl. "I think I'm the one to blame for G being distracted in class yesterday. She's been such a good friend to me, and I know that I could've done a better job at keeping her focused."

"That's just it, Mr. and Mrs. Reign," Mr. Reynolds interjects, stopping my word vomit from continuing. "I'm aware that it's become increasingly difficult for Georgia to focus in class, and yes, I know that her grades have dropped in her math class and in some of her other ones as well."

Georgia's eyes slowly become glassy, and she tries to explain. "It's not easy for me. You just don't get it, Mr. Chang."

"I'm trying to, Ms. Reign. That's why we're here."

Mr. Reynolds holds a finger in the air. "I think I can help. Georgia," he says, focusing solely on her. "How do you feel when you're in class, any class?"

"I mean...," she starts, then looks at me. I nod at her to keep going, hoping she can read my mind. *We're all here to support you.*

"Tell them what you texted me yesterday," I say, pulling out my phone when I remember that we recently talked about this very thing.

"You mean when I told you that I can't sit still and that when my teachers start explaining things, I always get lost, mostly because it all sounds like gibberish."

"Exactly. And what did you say about always getting detention?"

"Oh yeah. I said that it's not fair that I keep getting thrown in kiddie jail because I talk all the time in class. I can't help it. Like, I even try not to talk, but my body and my mouth do their own thing." She watches me, and I coax her to take a few really deep breaths. "What else am I supposed to do? Sit still for two whole hours and not say a word?"

"I mean...she does have a point," I agree.

"And maybe," she continues, "when I interrupt the other kids all the time it's because they take so long getting to the point. They always claim that I'm butting in, but I have things to say and I can't wait for them." I nod at her to keep going. She really is doing a good job expressing herself. "And sometimes I don't even want to interrupt, but I just can't stop myself."

"Makes perfect sense to me," I say, and slurp down a big gulp of my macchiato.

"Georgia," Mr. Reynolds asks. "Do you lose things often?"

"She'd lose her head if it weren't attached to her neck," Mrs. Reign says, patting Georgia's shoulder.

Mr. Reynolds leans closer to her. "Do you lose your keys? And your wallet?"

"And my homework," she whisper-admits, tugging at the thread on her sleeve. "And my books and pencils, too."

"All the time," I say. "I try to help keep those things in order for her."

Mr. Reynolds smiles and nods. "It's really good that you're there for her, Lyric, but I think there could be something else going on here. Something that needs even more support than her friends being there for her."

"Like what, Mr. Reynolds?" Georgia's dad asks, his eyes widening.

"Well, I know she struggles with finishing her classwork in my English class, and when I give them deadlines, she does her best to manage her time, but that's also been challenging for her."

"All facts," Georgia says, crossing her arms over her chest. "The work is cool, but being on top of the time thing is hard."

"I thought it was just her being twelve and that she'd grow out of it," Georgia's mom says, reaching for her daughter's hand. "Isn't all of this mostly growing pains?"

"Sometimes it can be, Ms. Reign, but in Georgia's case, I think there could be a deeper issue. I've had students go through the very same thing in the past few years, and it was more than just growing pains."

"So what are you saying?" Georgia's voice quivers. "That there's something wrong with me?"

"There's nothing wrong with her," I say, glaring at Mr. Reynolds, who I thought was here to help, but now I'm starting to question that.

"No. No." He clears his throat and puts both hands on his knees. "I think Georgia could really benefit from seeing a trained clinician, a therapist. If there's something happening besides just being a little messy and disorganized, we should use our resources and have a clinician let us know. Get our girl properly diagnosed."

Georgia picks at a scab over her knuckle. She whisper-asks, "Does that mean that I'm weird?"

"Not at all, honey," her mother says, soothing her. "You're perfectly you. But if Mr. Reynolds is right and there's something else going on, I think we need to address it and see. I've noticed all the things he's brought up today, and if you don't have to go through that, I'd like to get you the support you need to make everything easier."

"I'm in agreement, Mrs. Reign," Mr. Chang says. "I'd hate to fail her if I don't have to."

Georgia turns to our math teacher and declares, "I'm not dumb."

"We know that, kid," her dad says. "You remind me a lot of myself at your age."

"I know you're not dumb, too, G," I agree. "You're one of the smartest friends I have."

Georgia forces a smile. I know this can't be easy for her. I wouldn't want anyone telling me about my brain and how it does or doesn't work. But then, Mr. Reynolds says something that shifts the energy in the room.

"I can relate to everything you're going through. And it was only when I made an appointment and saw a therapist that everything made sense for me. And managing my life got easier."

"Really?" Georgia asks, tilting her head to meet his eyes.

Mr. Reynolds's face lights up, twinkling when he

smiles. "So. How about we make a plan to get her to a therapist and go from there?"

"You really saw one, too?" Georgia asks quietly.

"Sure did. And I know a really good one that one of my other students likes. Her name is Dr. Simone."

"Yessssss!" I pep, snapping my fingers like I've just figured it out. "My friend sees her and really likes her, too."

Georgia looks at her mom and then her dad. "Does that mean I'm not kicked out of the play?"

"Well, first, you have to agree to go to the therapist and see what's happening with you. You need to be in charge of you. And be committed." Her dad folds his hands in his lap and lowers his gaze to G. "Can you agree to that?

Georgia takes a long, deep breath, and after darting her eyeballs around the classroom a few times, she finally tugs on her cowboy hat and says, "Guess so."

"And it doesn't mean anything more than you have a whole tribe in this room rooting for you."

"And not failing you," Mr. Chang says, tossing the pop quiz into the wastebasket. "We believe in you. Now the ball is in your court." He turns to Mr. Reynolds and half smiles. "Thank you, Mr. Reynolds, for shining some light on our situation."

"Yeah, you're pretty cool, Mr. Reynolds," I say before turning to Georgia. But my heart goes out to my friend when she slumps deeper into her seat and whisper-fesses.

"Then why do I still feel like a failure?"

The next few days are a blur. Georgia and Twinkie worked overtime to find new followers for me. It was good for Georgia to focus on something other than her own stuff, too. They recorded me singing every song under the sun that matched my voice, but I only managed to gain a few hundred more. *American Rockstar* would never consider that a win, so we had to go back to the drawing board.

"I think this outfit will make a good one," Twinkie says on Thursday while we're in the thrift shop on Wilshire. She holds a fuzzy lion costume with a tattered mane in the air. "It'll be great for doing *The Lion King*."

"Ew!" I screech when I spin around and get a whiff of it. "Way gross."

"But it works," Twinkie says, egging me on. "You'll look adorbs in it. We can even muss your hair and paint whiskers on you, too."

I shrug. What's the point of fighting with them when they're only going to double-team me and force me into raggedy costumes for the Gram?

"The cheesier the look, the greater the chance of you going viral," Georgia explains.

"Yeah," Twinkie cosigns. "We're making reels this time, and since we're focusing on big songs from musicals, it'll be a smash. It just has to be."

"My voice is perfect for the teapot in *Beauty,*" I flex. "That song hits."

"Facts," Georgia says, bobbing her head, singing the first verse of "Beauty and the Beast."

"OOOOOH!" Twinkie shouts from the other side of the store. "This is it! Purrrrfect for *Annie.*" She dangles a little red dress in the air. "We're getting it. No conversation needed."

"But. It's yucky," I protest, throwing my hands in the air. "And ugly."

Georgia sucks her teeth and snaps back, "It's vintage. And cheap."

"And adorbs," Twinkie adds, grabbing my arm and leading me to the cash register. "You have to trust your manager. I know these things."

"We have all the looks we need for now. There's a witch costume in my closet that'll work for Glinda, and we already have—"

Twinkie holds a finger in the air and checks the list on her phone. "We have *Wicked, Annie, The Lion King,* and *Beauty and the Beast* covered. Let's get our American Rockstar into character and get this show on the road."

"I'm so not doing *Annie*!" I cross my arms. "Buy it if you want, but no! Nope! Nopers!"

Georgia's lips purse, and she scowls. "What's the deal?"

"Long story. Too much trauma to unpack today."

Ring it up, Twinkie mouths to the shop girl anyway.

It isn't even an hour later and we're in my backyard on the barnwood plank stage Dad built for my birthday last year. He insisted that stage presence was as necessary as Doritos on Netflix and Chips nights.

"Turn the lights on," Twinkie yells at Georgia, who is on a short ladder fiddling with the bulbs in the lighting mount. "We need her spotlighted."

Thanks to Dad, you wouldn't even know you were in my backyard once you walk past the pool. There's an outdoor theater, complete with proper lighting, sound, and even a backstage area. It's legit baller, thanks to the big money from Mom's monster hit, "Paper Cuts."

"How's that?" Georgia asks Twinkie, who is busy setting up the first shot.

"Perf!" Twinkie answers, shoving her thumb into the air and cuing the music.

I look toward the pool and see Aunt Jackie's bedroom light flicker on.

"Ready...set...and—" Twinkie points her index finger

at me as she circles the front of the stage. She holds the camera steady as she records my rendition of Annie's "Tomorrow." That's when she notices that I'm NAWT wearing the wig.

"Where's the rest of your costume?" she questions me, eyeing the red wig I found in Mom's closet that's not plopped on top of my head.

"It made me itch," I lie. "We're losing time," I say, trying to get the show on the road.

"Okay." Twinkie finally gives in. "Let's roll. The show must go on."

"You got this!" Georgia yells. "Sing your little heart out."

I do just that and crush that last, long, super infamous note of the song.

"Let's get her changed for *The Lion King*," Twinkie orders, checking the time. "We're making progress, people. Let's keep the momentum."

We race to get me ready to sing "Can You Feel the Love Tonight" in that nasty lion getup. It smells like someone stored rotten eggs in it, then decided to pee on it, too. Just...EW!

The outfit definitely didn't make me want to feel the love tonight. But I perform that song on the stage like my heart found its soulmate. Whenever I question what on earth I'm doing in that stinky getup, Twinkie just says, "How badly do you need followers?"

"Okay, I think that's a wrap," Twinkie finally says after she manages to get enough footage of me pounding out vocals from both *Wicked* and *Beauty.*

"I'm pooped," I say, taking off the awful teapot costume we threw together with scraps from Dad's closet.

"You were amazy. I think this will be the missing link we've needed to grab the world's attention."

"Plus, you look so darn cute," Georgia cosigns. "My fave was watching you perform the big song from *Annie.* That ratty wig would've been chef's kiss."

I shake my head into a serious objection. "Mom says it brings out her saucy side. Double yuck!" I say, plopping down on the stage to catch my breath.

"I'm uploading the last one now," Twinkie says, working magic on her cell. "And then let's sit back and wait for the love."

"I'm so glad you two are here," I admit. "I couldn't do this without you."

"That works both ways," Georgia says, matter-of-fact. "Thanks for bringing Reynolds in for that assist. Without you two, I probs wouldn't be in the play."

"You ready for therapy next week?" Twinkie asks Georgia.

"You ready to sing in front of the entire Valentine Middle student body?" G says right back at Twinkie.

Georgia flicks the front of her cowboy hat when I gasp. "Don't freak out, Lyric; I'm still going."

I find my zen and take off Dad's oversize boat shoes. "I see. Well, since your appointment is scheduled for four PM next Saturday, I'm thinking we hit play rehearsal, then we all three walk over to your session together."

"Good. Because if y'all actually thought that I was going by myself…"

I grin at her. "Never crossed my mind. Brooklyn says that having a buddy when she went the first few times helped her a lot. She's the one who goes to Dr. Simone."

Twinkie folds all the costumes into a neat pile and stops to focus on getting her point across. We walk to the pool and sit on the cabana loungers in silence. After a few beats, Twinkie suggests, "You should ask her about her experience. Maybe it could help."

"I do like the idea of having my friends there," Georgia answers, her cheeks shading pink as she looks away. Then she just says, "Maybe."

A mix of concern and compassion is in the air. It floats around for a bit then settles over the pool somewhere.

"Either way, we got you," I finally say, seeing Aunt Jackie's bedroom light go dark.

"We all have each other," Twinkie says, sniffling.

"Are you crying?!" I ask.

Twinkie swipes her cheeks. "It's just that... well... I can totally feel the love tonight."

I break out singing the song from *The Lion King*, and I feel the love, too. When I hit the last note, I realize I'm not the only one feeling it.

"That's a wrap. She's totally crying!" Georgia coos about Twinkie.

I catch my breath before explaining to her, "There's no crying in musical theater."

We all break out laughing because that's a blatant lie. Everyone knows there's *always* crying in musical theater.

CHAPTER 11

I'm feeling a mix of emotions the next week when Mom and Dad get back home. It's only that I've been able to move around easily with just Aunt Jackie keeping her one good eye on me. I hop out of bed as soon as my alarm screams at me to rise and shine. I don't know about shining, but I'm absolutely racing to get ready for school and out of the house before the parentals have a chance to talk to me. They got back late last night, and don't get me wrong, I'm psyched that they're home, BUT things are getting a little slippery and I need to slide right past them.

"Boogie! Boogie!" Mom stops me just as I'm heading out the front door. *Crud!*

"Hey, Mom," I say, not making eye contact. I stare at the peephole in the oversize front door, wishing I was on the other side of it.

"What's the rush, Boogie?"

"Oh…no rush. Just trying to stay out of your way. I know you've got tons to do to prep for the studio." I look everywhere but at her. "I respect the hustle."

"You're never in my way." I can feel Mom standing behind me, and I'm forced to turn around and give her my attention. She leads me back to the kitchen with her arm looped through mine. "Now. How's my favorite girl?"

My heart is thumping, and my palms are now wet with worry. "I'm groovy. Just heading out to meet Georgia and Twinkie for a latte before school."

"What's the haps with the play?" Mom asks, moving the wispy dirty-blond tendril from my right eye. "I need all the deets. I've been gone, and I know so much has happened."

She has no idea.

"Well, uh…we have rehearsals, uh, today and t-t-tomorrow," I stutter.

"You know your lines, Superstar?" Dad asks, walking into the kitchen and grabbing a piece of burned toast.

"Yep, most of them. I studied all last night while you two were on your way home."

"Boogie." Mom starts down the twisty yellow brick road. "I've been meaning to ask you something."

Uh-oh. Here we go.

"I can't seem to see any of your posts on Instagram anymore."

"Me either, Boogs," Dad says. "I'm starting to feel rejected."

It's at this very moment that I'm confronted with, well, me. Who do I want to be? A liar? A manipulator? A downright bad person?

Mom leans against the island and blows at the steam swirling around her coffee mug that reads BEST MOM EVER. Dad flips through the paper. And me? Well, I count backward from five trying to devise a plan.

"Every time I try to check your IG, it says no posts yet," Mom says after sipping her coffee.

"Did you delete all your beautiful pics, Boogie?" asks Dad. "Because they were all so adorable."

Here goes nothing.

"I, uh, don't know what you're talking about," I answer, heading for the front door. "I really have to go. The girls are waiting."

"Well, wait. How do we fix this IG thing?" Dad yells at my ponytail that's flying through the tension in the air.

"It must be an algorithm thing." I swing open the door. "Just a malfunction, some kind of bug in the system."

Aunt Jackie scurries into the kitchen, her morning wig hanging over her left eye. "I just came to get the piping-hot tea," she says, winking at me. "Don't you just hate those little buggers in the algorithm?"

My eyes lock with Aunt Jackie's. She tightens her orange housecoat with the lace trim and smiles slyly.

Mom yells after me. "We want to see what's going on in your world, especially with the play."

"I'll call Instagram today," I say, and slam the door behind me.

"You'll call Instagram?" Georgia says when we get to school. She's holding her belly, laughing so loud that my ears are ringing louder than the morning bell.

"What was I supposed to say?" I challenge her, walking toward my locker.

"How does one even call Instagram?" Georgia wipes the tears from her eyes. "That's classic."

"I couldn't think of anything else. It's like I was caught in a spiderweb, and the lies were starting to strangle me to death."

"Your mom is Jade Darby. She's no dummy. She'll know you blocked her."

"Maybe. But it's not like she manages her own socials, so my fingers and toes are crossed." I literally cross my fingers and wave them around my head to drive my point home. "I just need a little time."

"Ballsy," Georgia says. "I like it."

"I couldn't risk her seeing that we tagged *American Rockstar* in all those posts and reels. Besides, I only have a little more than four thousand followers at this point, and I need to really rev it up before auditions tomorrow. And the parentals canNOT see any of that."

Georgia stomps her cowboy heels into the floor and laughs some more. "I get it. But couldn't you have just told her that you deleted your IG?"

"She knows I love myself way too much to ever do something so tragic."

"I'll say," Georgia says, gawking at my locker, which I decorated with balloons, wallpaper, and streamers before school. It's a superstar theme and it's gorge! My entire locker is covered, and admittedly, some of it stretches onto my neighbor's, too. "What exploded over here?"

I snap a few pics of it and post it to the Gram before taking the small red rug out of my tote bag and laying it on the floor in front of me. "What do you mean?"

I open my locker to reveal pink-and-gold glittery wallpaper under a zillion framed pictures of me. I steady the mini chandelier and battery-operated string lights that are blinking around my gym clothes and math book. I stop and blow myself a kiss in one of the twenty mirrors taped to the inside of my door.

"O-M-Get out of town! Why does your locker look like Party City vomited all over it?"

"I still don't get what you're trying to say, G." I wave my arms up and down the side of my locker like a showgirl in a furniture store. "It's décor. A reflection of me. And I'm going to be a star!" I step back to admire it all. "And it's fabulous."

"It's... something," she says, still smirking.

"Judgy much?" I huff, pointing my finger at her OOTD. "I never say anything about that whole fake cowgirl thing you have going on."

"Now wait just one minute!" Georgia punches the air with her faux snakeskin cowboy hat. "Fake where?"

"G. You wear western gear every day! We live in the middle of Santa Monica. Two miles from the Pacific Ocean." I flip my hair over my shoulder. "Make it make sense."

"That hurts. Take it back."

I cross my arms. "Just saying."

"You're being selfish and... mean."

"I'm sorry, G. I didn't mean to be mean. It's just that

you're clowning my exquisite taste. My locker décor is *every*thing."

"No. I'm not. You're violating school policy. And you're clearly infringing on somebody else's personal locker space." She points to my neighbor's locker and clucks her tongue against her teeth. "That's just... rude!" Her attention shifts to the floor. "And you have a bathroom rug in front of it!"

"It's my red carpet." I fluff my curls in one of my many mirrors. "Duh."

"Well, your red carpet is against school policy, too. Your locker neighbor won't appreciate any of this. Trust me." She grabs my elbow and spins me around to look at her. "Not cute, Lyric."

I check out the pink-and-gold decorations that have spilled onto my neighbor's turf. "She'll be all right," I say, and reach for my English textbook.

"Seriously?" Georgia challenges me. "Think of somebody besides yourself. I refuse to let you become *that* girl."

"Fine!" I pick the streamers and wallpaper from the other locker and peel the tape away to remove the few metallic balloons. "Better?"

She eyes all the themed stuff that's still covering my locker. "I mean... I guess?"

From down the hall, Twinkie waves at us and then points at her watch. "C'mon!" she yells. "We're gonna be late!"

I close my locker and square with Georgia. "Sorry about what I said. Your western vibe is fire." She forces a smile, but still lets me link my arm with hers before we head down the hall and around the corner to English class.

I settle into my seat and watch the day creep by SO slowly. It's like it's deliberately taunting me. I'm simultaneously staring at the clock and also impatiently waiting for a text from Mom telling me those four dreaded words: *WE. NEED. TO. TALK.*

Luckily, they never come. But unluckily, I do get a different text from her:

> MOM: Looks like we have to jet out of town for a quick sec, Boogs. But promise it'll be super fast. Be back before you know it.

Again? You'd think I'd be used to feeling abandoned and rejected. But all I can say, despite feeling well, abandoned and rejected, is that I can move forward with my master plan.

* * *

After school, I run back into the building and bolt down the hallway, around the corner, and straight into the theater. I'm sweating and out of breath when I hear Mr. Reynolds's voice smack me in the face.

"Well, hello there, Lyric. So nice of you to join us."

I straighten my skinny tie and tuck my crisp white button-up into my plaid miniskirt. "I'm sorry, Mr. Reynolds. I know I'm late. I was just, uh, just uh—"

"She was checking on her grandmother," Georgia interjects from the stage. "She told me to relay the message, but I completely forgot."

The entire room is silent. Everyone is watching me. I watch them back, forcing a grin at the football players who are upstage working on the set. Then I wave to Magic and Brooklyn, who are leading the HoneyBees in a dance routine. They wave back, but not with their usual sugary, sweet flair. That's when I know I've let them down.

"You're an hour late. Maybe next time, tell your, uh, grandmother that you have a commitment on Fridays and Saturdays to Valentine Middle."

"Yes, you're right, sir," I say, tossing my stuff onto a chair in the audience, grabbing my script from my faux-leather messenger bag, and walking up to the stage. "I'm so sorry. It won't happen again." The kids in the back of the theater return to working on their songs with the music director, Ms. Pepper.

"Well, since you were dealing with your personal stuff, I had Stormy take over your role."

"I can take it from here. I'm here now." I put my palm in the air and promise. "And I'm not going anywhere. Pinky swear."

Mr. Reynolds moves upstage and takes Stormy with him. He bends down and says something to her that we can't hear. She spins on her heels and walks offstage without a fuss, but I can see that she's fuming. I totally get it. She wants this role, and I'm the only one standing in her way.

"Okay, Lyric. We were on page fifteen."

"It's me and you, kid," Georgia says, crossing her left foot over her right ankle. "I'm talking about how I'm finally going to get some brains when we ease on down the yellow brick road heading to Oz."

I flip through my script. "Got it. Yes. I'm all caught up."

"On second thought"—Mr. Reynolds loosens his tie—"let's take it from the top."

I'm thrilled to start from page one, but the rest of the cast doesn't seem to feel the same. I can tell because I hear a chorus of kids suck their teeth and groan.

"Everyone. Everyone." Mr. Reynolds walks downstage.

"Let's take five and get ourselves together and then take it from the top." He rubs his forehead. "We could all use a quick break."

"Where were you?" Twinkie asks, tugging on my shirt. "We didn't know if something happened to you."

Georgia yanks on my other sleeve. "Yeah, you gotta give a girl some notice next time so I can properly have your back."

We head to our seats, and they both dig through their stuff until they find their water bottles. Twinkie sips hers while Georgia guzzles loud enough for Stormy to turn around and scoff at us.

"It's all good," I whisper-explain. "I was just getting a few more reels done around campus. I shot this on the football field at the fifty-yard line, and this one here"—I pull up the footage and continue—"was me singing in the gym while the boys were practicing." I move through my videos and land on the last one. "And this was at the pool."

"Whoa!" Twinkie raves. "On the diving board."

Georgia shoves a toothpick into her mouth and nods. "You're really getting creative."

"I don't have much of a choice." I wince. "Tomorrow is the big day, and I need—"

"Five thousand"—Twinkie starts doing the math in

her head like a wiz—"two hundred twenty-six more followers."

"And a miracle," I admit.

"Let's go, cast. Time to take it from the top," Mr. Reynolds announces from center stage four minutes later. "Now that we have Lyric, let's move through act one and see how it all feels."

"You're up, L-Boogie," Georgia says, pushing me down the aisle toward the stage.

"Let me get Dorothy and Aunt Em onstage." Mr. Reynolds points to the wings. "And I'll need Uncle Henry and the Munchkins ready in the wings."

"Are we singing 'The Feeling We Once Had?'" I ask, stepping onto the stage and taking my mark.

"Not today. You'll be practicing that tomorrow with Ms. Pepper. We're lucky to have landed her. She's a retired *professional* musician." I like Ms. Pepper. In my mind, she resembles Little Miss Muffet, who, they told us, sat on a tuffet eating her curds and whey. Only Ms. Pepper eats string cheese and carrot sticks. I still don't know what a tuffet is—or curds, for that matter.

"I know the song already," Stormy Jackson brags from her front seat in the audience, snapping me back into rehearsal.

"I'm sure you do," I snort at her. She's so annoying, but it's not like I have any room to be huffy, considering I'm the reason we're a whole hour behind today.

"Thank you, Stormy. But I'm sure Lyric is ready, too." I watch the creases in Mr. Reynolds's smile fade when he says, "But don't stray too far. There are a lot of moving parts, so we might need you after all."

When Mr. Reynolds turns his back, Stormy charges to the aisle and up the steps to the stage. She grabs my script and stomps her feet into the hardwood.

"You're not cut out for this," she accuses me. "You're not committed. And I know why."

"What are you talking about?" I huff, snatching my script back from her.

"I follow you on Insta. I see what you're really doing."

"What I'm doing is prepping for act one in our school play. You know, the one where I'm playing the lead role, Dorothy." I take two steps away from her. "And you're not."

"Valentine Middle's production of *The Wiz* is no stepping stone to *American Rockstar*. And I'm offended that you would even put us in that situation."

"And what sitch is that, Stormy Jackson?" My bottom lip starts to twitch, but I bite into it and hold my breath. She's the last person who needs to know about my master plan. Well, the third—after Mom and Dad. I shake it off and stand my ground, dishing out more lies in one day than I have in my whole life. "What are you even talking about?"

"We are more than your little opportunity. We are a professional PRO-DUC-TION!"

I check out Ms. Pepper in the back of the theater working with the choir on one of the songs from the play. The kids are off-key and a few beats behind the music. They sound awful, TBH. I sigh, giving Stormy the last bit of attention I can muster. Even though she's right about me using our show for leverage, it's none of her beeswax. Fact: I'm going to have to keep a close eye on her and throw her off my scent; she already knows too much.

I move downstage, blocking her, and spew over my shoulder, "You're standing in my light."

CHAPTER 12

It's the biggest day of my twelve-year-old life because I'm finally stepping into the role I know I was always meant to have. There might be some deception happening in order for me to climb to the top, but President Barack Obama once said that progress is not a straight line and not always a straight path. If a man who was once the president of the United States understands that sometimes you must bend the rules to get where you're supposed to be, then my actions should actually be applauded. Right?

The next morning at play rehearsal it is time to do my favorite thing—sing. Mr. Reynolds decided this week to designate Fridays for blocking and Saturdays for songs and dances. Now, under normal circumstances, I would have been thrilled to beast my solos, but today I'm seriously anxious about my second *American Rockstar* audition. I'm going to have to perform on their stage in front of the producers, and my IG following isn't exactly where Bailey said I should be. As a matter of fact, I'm only halfway there. But I can't ruminate over that now; I don't want Mr. Reynolds or the entire cast of Valentine Middle's *The Wiz* to put me on ice, so I do my best and focus on the music in front of me.

"Lyric, I'm really impressed with your take on 'Soon as I Get Home,' but you make the room spin when you sing, 'Home.'" Ms. Pepper oohs and aahs from the piano that's positioned upstage. She'd given us each copies of all our music to take home and practice when the final cast list was posted. Honestly, I mastered most of my songs before auditions. I wasn't being presumptuous, I just knew them already—thanks to the parentals. When I was seven, Mom and Dad played the soundtrack to the musical for a whole month of my life. It was fate.

"Thanks, Ms. Pepper." I step back and take a bow. "I grew up on this stuff."

"Well. Your voice is beautiful, dear." She plays a few chords and then stops. "I think that's enough for now. Let's have our Lion step up with you to work on 'Mean Ole Lion' next."

My eyes dart over the heads of the cast in search of Twinkie. But I can't find her until Magic and Brooklyn slide to the side to reveal my mini manager crouching behind them, next to a few other Munchkins.

"Twinkie, come on over here," Ms. Pepper says, playing the intro to the song. "Let's see what you've been practicing at home."

"Oh, I haven't really, I mean..."

"She can barely read aloud in class, how is she going to sing in front of a whole audience?" A boy cackles from the crowd of kids. "She's a real scaredy-cat, just like the dumb Lion."

I turn around, searching for the bully. Then I spot him, leaning against a few props next to the football players, who are busy painting a set of foam bricks yellow.

Buster Brown.

Buster is known around Valentine Middle for being the school menace. He's always calling someone out, making them feel bad about themselves. It's become sort of his thing. Usually, the other kids laugh when he makes mean jokes, but I don't find it funny, especially now when his target is one of my fave girlies.

Georgia storms over to Buster and looks him square in his eyes. He backs down long enough for her to turn to Twinkie and reach for her hand. But it's too late. Twinkie's confidence is shaken.

"I'm not uh, very, uh—" Twinkie squeaks, her knees wobbling in place.

Georgia grabs her hand and leads her to the piano. She leans closer and whisper-encourages our Lion. "You can do this."

Twinkie's shoulders slump, and she breathes out fear. "But it's so hard."

"You can do hard things," Georgia reminds her.

I move to the other side of Twinkie and touch her shoulder. "Totally. Got. This."

Twinkie looks back and forth between Georgia and me. I really hope she doesn't start to cry. Then, the universe answers, and I watch her fill her lungs with courage... and sing.

Now, if I'm being honest, it isn't her best work, but it's obvious that our girl's got talent. Yes, it's buried right now. But it's still in there. Somewhere.

When Twinkie hits the second verse, she's doing her

best to show that she's mean and not to be messed with as she sings all about being savage, but then it happens.

♪♪ *You'll be standing in a draft*
If you don't hear me laugh

"You're not scary," Buster yells from behind me. "And you're definitely not mean."

Before he can say another word, Georgia crushes his Converse with her cowboy boot. Hard.

"OWWW!" he squeals.

When he looks up in agony, she shrugs. "Ooh, sorry. My bad. I didn't see you there."

But Twinkie saw him there AND heard him AND took it as her cue not only to stop singing, but to run off the stage, down the steps, up the aisle, and right out of the theater.

"You know, you don't always have to be a jerk, Buster," I snap, before turning to run after Twinkie.

If I know my Twinkie, she's hiding out in her safe space: the bathroom.

I swing open the door and peer under the stalls, checking for her rainbow-colored sneakers. "Twinkie, it's just me."

Georgia barrels into the bathroom a few seconds later. "And me."

"We only want to talk to you." I lean against one of the sinks and stare at the steel door that's shielding her from us.

"Or not talk." Georgia turns on the faucet and washes her hands. "Whatever you want. It's totally your world, little squirrel."

I check my watch. I don't have much time before I have to be at the Pier. After the massive line to get to the stages in tent village two weeks ago, I want to be early today to secure my spot. I don't have the luxury of waiting all night for my turn in the spotlight. Mom and Dad might get sus.

The bathroom is silent. Georgia glances at me, and I check my watch again. Then finally, the stall door opens and Twinkie slogs toward us.

"You okay?" I ask, opening my arms for her to fold into them.

She shakes her head.

"You can't let that kid get to you." Georgia bounces from side to side, holding up her dukes, ready for a fight. "Everyone knows he's a bozo. A total clown."

"But he's right," Twinkie mutters.

I hug her with one arm and wet a paper towel with the other.

She wipes away her tears with it. "I have no business trying to sing in front of a whole audience of strangers."

"You have just as much right as he does!" I yelp. "Who made him the king of the cast?"

Georgia's long, thick lashes flutter when she looks at Twinkie. It's in that uber-special, "we're best friends" sort of way. "Yeah, besides, your voice is one of the best out there. We just need to find a way to pull it out of you."

"You really think so?" Twinkie asks, not feeling the confident vibes.

"Nope," Georgia shakes her head. "I know so."

Then I have the most brillz thought. "How about we practice later? After my audition at the Pier and G's therapy session."

Georgia, full of energy, breakdances in the mirror. "I'm down for that. Count me in."

I lock eyes with Georgia, trying to telepathically calm her. Then I turn to Twinkie. "What do you say, Twink? We can get you ready. I promise." I hold up my pinky. "All you need is a little magic and some practice."

"Okay," she finally agrees, twisting her pinky with mine. "If you think it'll help."

"We're going to bring out that big bad Lion that's hiding inside of you." We snap our hands away and she smiles. "But now, I need to dip out of here."

"It does stink," Georgia says, waving her hand in front of her nose.

"No, not dip from the bathroom, but from school." I point to her Mickey Mouse watch and explain. "I gotta get to the Pier. I have to find Bailey and plead my case."

Twinkie checks the time on her phone, completely unaware that my entire life depends on this afternoon. "But we have another hour left of practice."

"We're going with you," Georgia says, always ready for the next adventure.

"No. You guys can just meet me there when you're done with rehearsal." I open the bathroom door and check the hallway to make sure the coast is clear. "Besides, your song is up next anyway, G."

"But you'll get in trouble," Twinkie says. "And they'll give your part to Stormy."

"If you two wow them with your musical genius, I bet they won't even notice I'm gone."

Georgia pops her collar. "I got this; I'll cover for you."

"Just not my grandmother again. You do know she's dead, right?"

Georgia thinks for a second before shaking her head. "RIP, Grandma."

By the time I get to the Pier, the line slinks from the parking lot where four small stages are set up next to tents, all the way up the Pier and onto Ocean Avenue. This time, however, the last person in line is posted up next to the Lobster restaurant, which isn't so bad.

I dash down the long ramp to the Pier and slide past tons of folks waiting their turn in the parking lot. Right away, I notice that the producers are wearing those same black tees with PRODUCER written in block letters across their hearts. Now if I could find one specific black tee with those life-changing letters.

"Have you seen Bailey?" I boldly yelp at one of them as he steps out of a tent.

"The line starts back there, kid," the balding guy says, pushing past me, right up to the stage where a boy is singing "The Star-Spangled Banner."

I jump up and down, trying to make eye contact with the producer. "But... I need to talk to her."

He signals for the boy to stop singing before turning back to me. "Back of the line like everyone else."

Ugh!

I try to get a sneak peek into the tents, searching for Bailey. But I don't see her anywhere.

Double ugh!

I trudge to the back of the line and wait behind a girl with a saxophone in one hand and a tambourine in the other.

And I wait.

And I wait some more.

An hour passes and I'm finally standing next to Bubba Gump Shrimp, in front of the stairs leading to the parking lot that's still transformed into a tent village.

"Hey! Lyric!" Georgia yells from behind a kid even shorter than Twinkie. "Lyric!"

I wave my hands in the air even though she's already spotted me.

"We came as soon as we could," Twinkie says, slinking through the crowd until she's standing beside me. "Sweet potatoes! We didn't miss your big moment."

My hands are a little slimy and my knees are starting to buckle. "Should be about a half hour more."

"Don't be nervous," Twinkie peps. "Remember what you told me: You got this."

"You're right," I admit, trying to refocus my attention to something that won't make me want to pass out. "So, dish the haps on the last hour of rehearsal."

Georgia and Twinkie eye each other.

"Well," Georgia starts. "I didn't mention your dead grandmother."

"Perf," I exhale.

"But please tell me you do have an uncle. Who is alive."

"No!" I yelp. "My folks are both only children."

Georgia smacks herself in the head. "I really gotta learn more about your peeps."

"What happened?" I yip.

"Well," Georgia starts, before racing through the sequence of events leading up to the big moment. "And then Mr. Reynolds wanted to hear us all sing 'Ease on Down the Road' at the end of practice, and you—"

"Stormy Jackson. That's it. That's the caption," Twinkie finishes.

I palm my forehead and close my eyes until I hear, "You're up next, kid."

Georgia pushes me down the last step and up to a long table next to a big banner that has AMERICAN ROCKSTAR written all over it. "That's you. It's your turn."

"Show me your platinum ticket," that same producer who banished me to the back of the line demands.

I panic for a quick second until I remember that I stashed it in my messenger bag toward the back of my English textbook so Mom wouldn't find it.

"Here you go," I say, handing it over.

He realizes that Georgia and Twinkie are part of my support squad and motions for them to step aside and wait for me. "Right this way, kid."

He leads me into a tent where I fill out a stack of

paperwork and show him the form with Mom's signature. Well, technically, it's my version of Jade Darby's signature, but who's comparing? And remember, President Obama would've done the same thing. I'm pretty sure.

"You're all set, Lyric Darby," he says, and sends me into another tent.

"Hi, I remember you," Bailey the producer says when I walk inside.

I feel lighter somehow. "Hey! Hey! You're Bailey." Just seeing her pie-shaped face restores my faith. Maybe I can advance without that monster following after all.

"That's me. All day, every day." She picks up her pen and scribbles something on the paper in front of her. I squint and see that my name was typed at the top. "I was hoping you'd show up today, Lyric Whitney Houston Darby."

"Wouldn't miss it..." And then I squeak, "For the entire world."

My mouth is dry. Like, really dry. It feels like I've been chewing cotton balls. I hate when this happens. It's not a common occurrence, mostly when I'm about to do something that will ultimately shift my universe. I get that I'm only twelve, but a lot can happen to a girl in twelve years, especially when she's fighting for her tomorrow.

"Well, Lyric. You're up. Let's hear what you've got." She

ushers me to the stage and points at the white X that's taped to the hardwood floor. I take my position and look out at the set of lights and cameras that are focused solely on... me.

"What song are you singing? Our pianist is world-class. Can rock with whatever you've prepared."

"Like... now? Just like that?"

"We've got this whole thing down to a science." She smiles at me and nods at the X. "Just like that."

I step onto the stage and tell him "Home" by Charlie Smalls or Quincy Jones. "Either version works."

He nods and then the music starts.

Just like that.

I take a deep breath.

And then I take another one.

And then I close my eyes and picture Mom standing beside me singing to me like she did the time I was in the hospital the day my grandmother died. Mom and I sang this song to her, and Dad said we called the angels who came to take her home to heaven. She'd been in a coma and hadn't spoken a word in months. But when she heard my voice hit the last note, she murmured the word "Home." Dad swore he saw her smile before she took her last breath and left us here to finish what she started.

"Wow, Lyric!" Bailey says when I take my final bow.

I'd gotten so lost in the memory of my heritage that I completely lost track of space and time. Mom says that happens to her sometimes. I only hope it was enough to get me to the next round.

"Come on down. Join me in the next tent," she says, pointing to the one beside the stage that a few teenage girls with septum rings are exiting.

"Was that good enough?" I ask, my eyes saucering. Behind her I can see a stack of gold tickets that say ROUND 3.

"You're one of the bigger voices we've heard this year. And to be so young. AND sooo good." She stops and looks at me like she's trying to figure out one of Chang's really hard math equations. "I think... you'd be a great fit for the show." Then she says it. "How's your IG following?"

"It's, uh, fine."

She scribbles something on her clipboard and asks, "At least 10k?"

When I don't answer, she looks up from writing and asks again. "Ten thousand minimum?"

"Well, not exactly," I admit. "More like 5k."

"I see," she says, setting the clipboard onto a round table beside a bunch of forms. Then she takes a deep breath and pinches her lips.

"It's just that I want this more than anything in the entire world."

"I understand," Bailey says, crossing her arms. "This is a big deal."

"I've been waiting my whole life for this opportunity."

"You can always come back next year. You know, when your numbers are up."

"It has to be this year. I can't go through another twelve months without a record deal."

"Lots of people want this, Lyric. See, the thing is that production has an unwritten rule about using socials to help the show gain traction. Basically, to get eyes on us. On our show."

"And I get that." I start to feel the tears stinging my eyeballs. I sulk, allowing them to fall down my face sloppily. "Jade says that all the time when she's doing stuff to make her songs go viral."

"Jade?"

"My mom. Jade Darby. She's always going on about how her socials are her bread and butter. She even hired a girl to help her manage them."

"Jade?" Then Bailey steps closer to me and squints her eyes. She repeats Mom's full name with emphasis, like she's swallowing it whole. "As in JADE *DARBY*?"

"Yeah, that's my mom. And she's obsessed with her TikTok." I catch the tears as they fall and think about the last time Mom tried to post the latest dance challenge to her page. Then I find my smile because Mom has that effect on me. I explain it to Bailey since she wasn't there. I make sure to use her real name because it's obvi having some kind of persuasive effect.

"One time, Jade kept falling when she was trying to make a video. See, she was wearing these sky-high stilettos with a super pointy heel. For the life of her, she couldn't balance herself. It was so funny. I couldn't hold the phone still anymore. I laughed so hard that she took the phone and made Elvis record her. But he laughed, too, so she had to dance and hold the phone herself. It was a nightmare." I'm holding my belly from laughing. "But it went viral, all right."

"Jade Darby?" Bailey asks again, just to make sure. "And Elvis Darby? From Love, Jade?"

"It was actually pretty funny. You know, cuz she's old."

"Well, this all might be a game-changer, Lyric."

"Why?"

"There's a real story here. Jade Darby's daughter on *American Rockstar*. I can see it now." She turns and gawks at me. "The story practically writes itself!"

Uh-oh. I'd been doing my best to showcase the fact that I come from singing royalty to get in good with the show, but I didn't anticipate it being splattered all over social.

"That's me," I pep, sniffling back fear. "I'm the one and only."

"Well, let me see what I can do about helping you get your followers up. You have two more weeks before you're in front of the judges. That's when they'll ask about your credentials. They'll also want to know about your experience. But since you're, you know, you, I don't think that matters so much anymore." She sizes me up like she just won the lotto. "We might be able to make some real magic happen by then."

I have no idea how I'm going to keep this from my mom now. She'd kill me if she found out I did all this without her permission.

But my dreams are worth it.

So I hold my hand out anyway, and Bailey gifts me a golden ticket that says I'm one step closer to making it all happen:

AMERICAN ROCKSTAR
ROUND 3

CHAPTER 13

"I don't want to do this!" Georgia sulks into the cushy chair in the waiting room outside the therapist's office.

"Sometimes we have to do hard things," I say, waving the golden ticket around.

As promised, after auditions, we went with Georgia to see Dr. Simone. At first, Georgia was on board, riding the day's wave of excitement with us, but as we got farther away from the sparkly ocean and closer to the brick building on Wilshire, her attitude changed.

"But you're not the one who has to go in that room and talk to a complete stranger about not being able to focus

OR sit still OR finish homework." I watch her slouch her shoulders and drown in a barrel of pity. Then she whisper-sighs, "It's, well... it's embarrassing."

"Nothing about you is embarrassing," Twinkie says, patting Georgia's left knee. "I totally get it. I should probs be in there, too, talking to her about why I can't sing in front of people. Sometimes, I can't even talk either."

"That's different, Twinkie," Georgia huffs.

"Uh... nope." Twinkie's head drops. "Not really different—AT ALL."

"I'm proud of you for being here," I say to Georgia, even though she's determined to not make eye contact with either of us right now. She's fixated on the beige Berber carpet, and I get it; the carpet won't judge her. "I know it's not easy, but just think, this way your teachers won't fail you and you can still be in the musical with us."

"I just wish I had some of your Sasha Fierce vibes, Lyric. You're all Yoncé in the making out there. And me, well, I'm—"

"You're—"

"Georgia Reign!" the cool-looking therapy lady announces, stepping into the waiting room.

"That's us," I say, standing up and extending my hand to her. I check out her short, coily hair and approve of the purple metallic bow tie that matches her purple-and-orange socks.

"It's nice to meet you, Georgia," the lady says. "I'm Dr. Simone."

"Oh." I take a step back and turn away from her. "I'm not Georgia."

Twinkie stands, pulls Georgia from the chair, and presents our BFF. "This one right here . . . she's the one and only."

Dr. Simone extends her hand. "Well, hello there, Georgia. You can follow me into my office. We can hang for a bit and talk."

After way too many deep breaths, Georgia finally breaks her staring contest with the carpet and looks at Dr. Simone. But since she doesn't say anything, a really awkward silence fills the room.

I nudge her forward. "When you're done, we can go to Cheesecake Factory. Twink and I will hang here till then," I offer, hoping the deliciousness and us not leaving our fave girlie will give G a boost. Instead, she turns to me and scrunches her face into a tight frown. I know that look. It's the one she always wears when she wants us to know that she's absolutely miserable. And I get it. Since third grade, Georgia has never opened up to anyone about this. We all know it can get hard for her, but to be honest, each of us has our thing. But we kind of move through the halls of Valentine Middle like we're doing just fine. It seems so much easier than being judged. Or teased. Or bullied because we're not perfect.

Why are we like that?

"Do you ever feel like you can't open up about your stuff?" Twinkie asks as Dr. Simone closes the door behind Georgia.

I plop into the chair. "I was just thinking about the exact same thing."

"Why do you think we don't talk about the hard stuff?"

"I dunno." I shrug, thinking about how I feel whenever Mom goes on tour with Dad, and I'm left all alone... abandoned. They're leaving tomorrow morning for another weeklong thing, this time around Barcelona, and I'm already having all the feels. I take a deep breath and admit, "It's just so much easier to pretend it's not there and push it all down."

"But then where does it go?"

I shrug again. "I'm not the expert with these things, but I do know that in science class we learned that a volcano erupts when pressure builds inside of it."

Twinkie taps her chin with her glittery nails. "Ahh, yes. So, we're like the magma."

"I know I don't want my emotional gas bubbling to escape. And then...BOOM!" I pop my hands over my face into an explosion.

"Whoa. That's deep."

"Am I standing in the light?" Twinkie asks later that night from my backyard stage. I promised her that I'd help her practice, and after a bit of tugging and tons of pulling, I got her on that stage. My thinking is that if she can conquer performing in front of the grass, trees, and pool chairs, then she'd be ready for all the soccer moms that would surely fill the theater on opening night. At least my backyard audience wouldn't boo her.

"Yes, you're standing in the light and you look divine," I tell her as she fidgets with her charm necklace. "You got this, I mean it. Now let's run it from the top of the song." I cue "Mean Ole Lion" and point my finger at her to start. And she does, but she definitely doesn't sound scary or mean. *Sigh.*

"Keep going," I encourage her. "But put a little more oomph behind the words. You know, like you're telling Buster Brown where he can shove it." I can tell she's trying because her eyes are all squinty and her eyebrows are crawling around her forehead when she spits out the words.

♪♪ *You'll be standing in a draft*
If you don't hear me laugh

But when she sings the part about threatening to knock them down if they make her frown cuz she's a mean ole lion, well, let's just say that it looks like my girl has the chicken pox!

I'm standing in the grass watching her scratch at the air and squirm around in her jumper. I can't for the life of me figure out what the exasperated expression on her face is supposed to relay to her audience. Even the pool chairs look confused.

"Stop! Stop!" I yell, waving my hands above my head to dead the noise.

"Was I abysmal? Like, really, tragically abysmal?"

"No, you weren't that bad," I hear a raspy voice say from behind me.

"Brooklyn!" Twinkie yells from the stage, wriggling her fingertips in the air.

"Your parentals are packing for tour. Your Aunt Jackie let me in. She's a live one, huh?" Brooklyn giggles as she sidles up to me and rests her elbow on my shoulder. "And Twinks wasn't that bad. Right, Lyric?"

"Not that bad at all," I agree. "But let's keep it cute, she could use some work." I wink at Twinkie. "But overall, I see the potential."

Twinkie shakes out her hands. "I don't know how to thank you for helping me, Lyric. I'd be lost without you."

"We'll practice every day if you want. I got you, girl."

"See," Brooklyn tells her, taking the few steps on the side of the stage two at a time. "You'll get there, and you'll be so mean I bet you'll be scaring off those pool chairs before you know it."

Twinkie slumps onto the stage floor and sits crisscross applesauce. When Brooklyn crouches down beside her, I decide now is a good time to take five.

"I guess we're taking a break, Twinks," I say, heading up the steps to join them.

"It really does get greater later," Brooklyn is saying to Twinkie when I plop onto the floor. "That's something my dad always says." She looks up at me and explains. "It's true, too; I mean, you should've seen Magic and me when we first got to Planet Pom-Poms Cheer Camp last summer."

"Were you two tragic like me?"

"Let's just say we're not called the Stumbles for nothing," she states, matter-of-fact. "But it got greater later, and now we're crushing it on the court." Then she laughs. "Most of the time."

Twinkie huffs, then looks Brooklyn in the eye. "So, what you're saying is that there's hope for me?"

"Yes, mama; there's hope for you."

Twinkie seems relieved, but I know how much practice she's going to need, and I'm counting on her being up for it.

"And there's hope for G, too," Brooklyn says, turning to me. "Thanks to you two."

I immediately put on my detective hat. "What have you heard?"

Brooklyn giggles before she says, "I came over to tell you that you two are the kind of friends everyone needs."

"Agreed," I answer. "But specifically... why?"

Brooklyn stops giggling and then takes a long, deep breath. "I honestly don't know what I would've done without Magic by my side in Dr. Simone's office. That waiting room can be so overwhelming."

"Ohhhh," Twinkie says, connecting the dots. "So, Georgia must've told you about therapy."

"Yeah, she texted to ask a few questions after her appointment today. She knows I'm going to therapy with Dr. Simone to help with all my sticky stuff." She shrugs, her wide smile spreading across her face. "And she might've told us that she had her squad there with her." Brooklyn is careful not to reveal anything they shared, but she does say, "I think you two are pretty cool. I thought I'd swing by and tell you in person."

"That's what friends are for."

"Yeah, but therapy is hard. It can be terrifying, too, especially in the beginning."

"I just hope it helps," Twinkie says, picking at her cuticle. "Cuz G deserves the best this world has to offer."

"It's really helped me deal with losing my mom and with my anxiety." She looks at me. "I know you're not really into talking about your personal business, Lyric, but I'm beginning to think that everyone should be in therapy. I've learned that it's not just for when you have problems."

"Preach, sister." Twinkie nods.

"It's cool when she helps me just process my days, especially when I've had a hard one. And some days are just hard."

"I get that," I admit. "I just dunno about getting so personal and . . . and—"

"Vulnerable," Brooklyn finishes for me. "It's not easy at first, but in the end, it helps with your mental fitness cuz I'm sure you have stuff you could share with someone like Dr. Simone." Brooklyn pulls her long goddess braids out of her hoodie. "We can all use more tips and tools to help us get closer to our happy."

Twinkie smiles. "I like that…getting closer to my happy."

"I guess," I say, thinking about Mom being on tour again and how all the crappy feelings and stinkin' thinkin' are running wild around my insides. "I'm pretty disappointed and mad at Jade Darby right now. I don't really want to look at her." Then I stop and put up my wall again. It helps me feel safe to hide behind it. So I finish by saying coolly, "It's no big deal. But yeah, you can call that stuff my sticky. I guess."

"And see, that's def something you should be working through with a profesh like Dr. Simone, Lyric."

"I'm good. I don't need to talk to anyone. I got it," I say, even though I know I don't. Lately, I haven't really had an appetite, and if I'm being honest, I haven't really slept like I normally do these last few weeks. But I could never talk badly to someone about Jade Darby; she's epic. And she's mine. "Nobody would understand anyway."

Brooklyn scoots closer to me. "That's what I used to say about my grief."

"But this is different," I say.

"Look." Brooklyn watches me, narrowing her eyes. Then she rests her palm on my knee. "I know that the whole mother-daughter relationship can be, well, complicated. I watched a few TikTok videos about it on Betty

Jean's account. So, see, I know what I'm talking about." She snaps her fingers to make sure we know her sources are legit. "And, Lyric, farealz, I'd give my entire hand to spend five more minutes with my mom. Don't take one second for granted being mad. If talking to someone will help you figure it all out, then it's worth it." She sniffles then says softly, "Actually, I'd even settle for two minutes."

I watch her eyes dart to the floor. And I don't say anything to drive my point home. I don't say anything at all.

"You're lucky to have your mom," Brooklyn says after a few long minutes. "I don't know if you understand just how lucky."

"I do."

Brooklyn gets up and dusts off her red joggers with the stripe down the side. "I'm out," she says, heading down the steps, a few tears following her.

"I'd trade places with you so fast," she says over her shoulder when she gets to the grass. "Whatever's going on, give your mom some grace."

Then she walks away, sniffling loud enough for me to know she left her heart on the stage with Twinkie and me.

CHAPTER 14

Monday morning, I wake up bright and early ready to talk to Mom about some of the things I've been feeling. Brooklyn was right; I'm lucky to have her and I don't want to take one second for granted. However . . . I quickly change my mind when I see the series of texts from Twinkie telling me that my life did just EXPLODE.

> 5:15 AM TWINKIE: Did you see the video?
>
> 5:18 AM TWINKIE: Are you up yet?

5:32 AM TWINKIE: OMG! OMG! Text me back!!

5:41 AM TWINKIE: CHECK YOUR INSTA. It's bananas.

5:47 AM TWINKIE: You're going viral.

5:56 AM TWINKIE: You're an overnight star!!!!

6:00 AM TWINKIE: You're totally INSTAFAMOUS!!!!!

I pick the sleep crust from around my eyelashes and open the app. Then I see it, right there in the palm of my hand.

American Rockstar posted my latest audition video—and tagged...ME!

I watch the video over and over of me singing my heart out, my mouth gaping open wide enough for a baby elephant to stomp into it.

This can't be real.

I check my following: 23,263 followers—and growing! At this rate, I'm a shoo-in for the show. Bailey said I only needed 10,000 followers, and I'm already way past that!

There's no reason why I shouldn't be able to compete for that record deal. On NATIONAL television!

EEK! I squeal, kicking my feet around in the bed.

6:03 AM TWINKIE: Did you see it
yet?! TEXT MEEEEEEEEE BACK!!!
PUH-LEASEEEE

Twinkie is seriously blowing up my phone, but she'll have to wait. It's finally ALL ABOUT ME. I get it, though. She knows what everyone else is finally realizing.

I.

AM.

A.

STAR.

A rising icon. A diva.

Yes, I'm aware that divas can get a bad rap out here in *The Industry*. But truthfully, the world loves divas. My namesake, Whitney Houston, was a legendary one.

Now it's my turn.

Jade Darby says divas know their value and that men put all that negative stuff on them because they're women. Her favorite line is "If Prince was a woman, they would have called him a diva, too."

"Lyric Whitney Houston Darby!"

Yikes! I know that tone.

That's when it hits me. I check the post again and slow down long enough to read what it says.

> @JADEDARBY'S DAUGHTER COULD
> BE THE NEXT AMERICAN ROCKSTAR.
> #legacy

"Lyric, get down here right now," Mom orders from the bottom of the stairs.

This can't be good, I think, wishing they'd hit the road for tour one hour earlier.

"In the bathroom," I say, jumping out of the bed and racing down the hall, past Aunt Jackie, who is standing in her doorway in a checkered housecoat with feathers, her hot tea in hand. She watches my every move. Then she blows at the vapors swirling around her chamomile and smiles.

I race past her, take the world's fastest shower, and hop out. Still wet, I tiptoe back to my bedroom. I have to escape the house before Mom has a chance to make it all go away. I can hear her on the phone with her manager going over this morning's flight info, so I close the door and check Insta again: 24k!

I grab my pillow and smush it into my face, screaming my head off.

I'm a total, complete, utter star.

Now I must dress like one, I think as I pull out my flashiest outfit that screams LEGEND. Perf!

I slip down the stairs and out the back door, determined to avoid Mom. There's no way she hasn't seen the post; it's a viral sensation. And let's not even get into the fact that they TAGGED HER! I bet that's why her manager called, to alert her that her kid is on stage crushing it in front of real-life Hollywood producers.

"Get back here, Lyric!" Mom screams from the front porch, stopping me before I sneak past her Range Rover in the driveway. "You have some explaining to do."

There's no use in hiding anything now. It's all out in the open. Mr. Reynolds always says that what's done in the dark will eventually come to light. I shove my sunglasses up my nose because right now the light is blinding.

"Lyric! I'm NAWT playing with you, YOUNGGG LADYYY."

Yep. She means business. I can always tell when she uses those two cringe words. "Coming, Mom."

I trudge back into the house and take a seat at the kitchen table, where she's waiting for me. The last time I got in trouble was when I ran up an outrageous bill on three different delivery apps. Mom and Dad were on the road for a weekend gig, and I was home alone.

That Saturday, I got hungry—like, *really* hungry. Since I couldn't decide what I wanted to eat, I ordered everything. This all happened before I became a part-time vegan, so there was a lot of pizza from Fat Sal's involved—obvi. The bill came to over two hundred dollars, and the parentals were not happy about it. They took my phone, moved Aunt Jackie and all her housecoats in, and put me on a budget. Thank goodness Dad helped me pay it all back. I can count on him to always come to my rescue.

"How did this happen?!" Mom demands to know. I get dizzy watching her wave her phone around in the air, right before it starts to ring.

She glances at the number and then huffs. Most calls are of the utmost importance for Mom. Everything is always about her career, and it usually needs to be handled immediately. I tap my pink-and-green press-on nails against the table and look past the island, avoiding Mom's death stare when she answers the call. That's when I spy Dad, poking his head into the kitchen. We lock eyes while Mom is jabbering to her manager about the weather in Spain during the two weeks she'll be there. It's only when Dad points to his phone and grins that I understand. He knows what I've done, and not to get ahead of myself here, but it looks like he's on my side.

When he shoos me toward the front door, I don't waste another second sitting there, waiting for my punishment. Instead, I grab my backpack and make my escape while he walks out the back door.

"Dad!" I yelp once we're both outside standing in the driveway. "She's, like, really mad."

"And she should be," he says with a degree of gruff in his voice that makes me nervous.

"Wait." I cross my arms over my chest. "I thought you were on my side."

"I am, Boogie. But you can't go sneaking around entering yourself into these big things when you know she doesn't approve."

"Yeah, but she doesn't understand." I look at the half smile that's spreading across his face. "You get it, don't you? Daaaddd?"

"I do. I know how much this means to you, and it wouldn't be fair if I didn't support you the same way I support her." He puts his arm around me. "But you have to do this the right way—with your mom on board."

"But she'll never let me grow up. I'm ready to start my career. I have over twenty thousand followers right now all because the biggest singing show in the world posted me. Me, Dad. Me!"

"The world is seeing what I've known all along."

"Why can't she see it, too? She was my age when she started singing backup."

He takes a long, deep breath. Then he finally says, "And that might have something to do with it, Boogs." He moves my flyaways and plants a kiss on my forehead like he always does when my world is ending. "I'll talk to her."

"You will?"

He shakes his head, and I breakdance in place. "Thanks, Dad."

"Now, get to school. We'll sort all of this when we get back in town." He glances at my outfit. "But why are you wearing a fur jacket? It's seventy-five degrees out here."

"Have a good tour," I say, ignoring his fashion review. "And say hi to Barcelona for me. Maybe bring me back something fancy. Maybe some Spanish leather."

"I thought you were a vegan."

"C'mon, Dad; not when it's in the name of fashion."

I turn to walk away, but he stops me.

"Hey, Superstar, I know you're not a little girl anymore, but I'm still your dad and I always wanna be first in line to get my goodbye kisses."

I spin back to him, standing on my tiptoes to smooch

his scruffy cheek. "You know you'll *always* be first in line. And thanks... for talking to Mom."

"Wish me luck. It isn't over yet." He rubs the back of his neck and shakes his head in disbelief. "You really went out there and auditioned. All by yourself."

I break into a wide smile as he turns to walk away.

"And you crushed it."

I yell after him. "Means a lot coming from you."

"You're growing up," he says, spinning around. "Right before our eyes."

"That's the plan, Dad."

"Well. I think it's hard for her." He swipes the tears from his eyes. "And for me."

"But I'll always be your little girl."

Dad stands beside the front door and sighs. "No, Boogie. You're becoming who you're going to be. And I'm so proud of it all."

"Dad! Are you crying?"

"My eyes... they're just leaking. They've been doing that more often lately."

"Thanks, Dad," I sigh back at him. I want to tell him to hurry back because I don't want to deal with all the negative emotions that show up when they leave. But I watch him fight with a few sniffles, and I change my mind. Instead, I send him all the good vibes, slowing down to pour on a little extra special sauce. "Have a great trip."

I walk backward toward the sidewalk and blow him a kiss, missing him already. Yes, it's true that I hate when they leave me to go on tour, but this time I have one cool thing to comfort me. Followers!

CHAPTER 15

I'm hiding behind my locker, waiting for all the kids to file into Ms. Pepper's homeroom class. When I spy Magic and Logan walk through the door, I grab my messenger bag and waltz into the room like I deserve a camera crew. My Insta has hit over twenty thousand, and I can't help but feel untouchable. I push my sunnies up my nose and shake out my big blond curls. Earlier this morning, I took the time to clip in my curly blond extensions so my hair would vibe with my new attitude. I brush them over my shoulders and glide to my seat.

"OMG, check her out," a girl's voice shrills.

Out of my periphery, I see the kids staring and raving. *It's all so EPIC.*

"Did you check out her Insta?"

"She's on *American Rockstar*."

"And they LOVE her."

"I heart her, tooooooo!"

I don't dare make eye contact. Stars are meant to be revered, so when I take my seat at my desk, I cross my legs and snuggle into the fur on my coat like I don't have a care in the world—even though it itches, and a small rash is starting to spread around my wrist.

"Lyric! We did it!" Twinkie says from the seat beside me. "We're going viral and getting all the followers you need to compete."

"*I'm* getting all the followers I need to compete," I correct her, fully embracing the diva that's been locked inside of me. Me. ME. I didn't know it would feel so delicious having it be all about me. But a girl could get used to this.

"That's what I meant," Twinkie says. "You're getting all the followers."

Sorry to be harsh to Twinkie, but I read somewhere that this is how Mariah Carey gets down. And the entire world loves her. Soon, they will love me, too.

"Well, we were there with you," Georgia says, her eyebrows darting into her forehead.

"I mean. Yeah, sure." I shift in my seat. The rash is moving up my arms, but I don't dare take off this darn fur.

"Hey, Lyric, will you sign this for me?" Magic shoves a torn piece of paper at me. I take it, realizing that it's from her math worksheet. I flip it over and sign my name. Then I just stare at it. I know my John Hancock is going to be worth some serious coin one day.

I pass my autograph back to her, and she coos at it. "Your song was amazy. I know you're going to win *American Rockstar* and be a big hit."

Yep. I was right. I'm hooked. Fame works for me.

Georgia steels herself, perking up her senses like a predator in the wild. "You canNAWT be serious." Her words pounce all over my shine before she turns to Twinkie. "Is she serious right now? Like, really serious?!" Georgia's eyes narrow when she nudges Magic in her rib cage. "What are you doing? That's not some random celeb; that's your friend. Lyric Darby."

"Yeah," Magic says, plopping into the seat in front of Georgia. "But she's Instafamous now. And that's, like, so stinking cool."

Georgia guffaws LOUDLY, rolls her eyes at Magic, and shrugs. "Whatevs."

"I'm so excited for you," Twinkie says while Ms. Pepper crunches on a carrot and gathers the papers on her cluttered desk at the front of the room. "Your whole life is going to change."

I smile to myself and reach across the aisle to pat Twinkie on her shoulder. "It's already ultra fab." I can see all the kids gawking at me and taking pictures on their cell phones. I don't let on that I'm actually in the middle of a crisis, still dodging Mom and her inevitable punishment, which I know will involve snatching me right out of the competition that made me Instafamous. But none of that matters right now since Mom is out of the country for a few whole weeks. I can revel in my fame until she gets back, and by then, I will have wowed the judges with my spectacular talent. And after that? A spot on the live show to sing in front of millions. There's no way she'll take that opportunity away from me. At least . . . I hope not.

"So, I signed up for group therapy with Dr. Simone this morning," Georgia says when the bell rings after homeroom. "I know Brooklyn said she likes the one-on-one with Dr. Simone, but me . . . not so much. I'm thinking being with other kids might be the secret sauce for me. When I told Brooklyn, she said therapy isn't really a one-size-fits-all kinda thing. But I'm still trying." I smile at her as we head to lunch, but she winces, popping the purple-and-cream suspenders over her denim shirt. "I mean, since you never asked."

"Cool. Cool. Cool," I say back to her, wondering why she's being so snarky today.

"It would've been the nice thing to do." Georgia pushes harder, trying to balance a stuffed notebook and a slew of papers in her arms. "I mean, a true friend would have asked about the biggest thing happening in *my* life."

"I did ask," I say, honestly not remembering if I did or didn't. I've just been so consumed with me and my fans today. I make a mental note to do better.

Georgia loses her grip on the mountain of stuff in her arms, and some of the papers fly through the air. She tries to grab them, but the notebooks tumble to the floor. "Uh, no. You didn't. You didn't ask. Not one time."

"Well, I thought I did," I lie, trying to save face.

"Lyric just has a whole lot going on right now," Twinkie says, taking out her phone to record me walking down the hall. When I see the other kids take out their phones to join her, I fluff my curls and walk ahead of Georgia.

"Why are you walking so fast?" she asks, trying to gather all her stuff.

"Because you're in my light," I explain, nodding at all the cameras pointing at my face. "Go ahead and push that FOLLOW button," I say to the gaggle of girls in the hallway stalking my Insta.

"You're seriously tripping," Georgia says, motoring to

catch up. She grabs my elbow to slow me down. "What's your deal? And why on earth are you wearing sunglasses inside?"

"That's what celebs do," Twinkie says to her, glancing over her phone. "It's a whole vibe."

"And I'm here for it," I say, turning to wave at my fans and then heading into the cafeteria.

Before Georgia has a chance to protest any louder, I grab her sleeve and face her. "Things are different now, but that doesn't mean I don't love you. Just be happy for me."

"I am. But you have to admit, all of this"—she points to the kids in the hallway who are still shadowing me—"is out of nowhere."

"All of this"—I blow kisses at my fans—"is what I've been waiting my whole life for."

"You don't have to act like this to enjoy your newfound fame," Georgia crows, spinning in the opposite direction. Then she stomps her cowboy boot into the floor. "But I do have one question."

"Of course I'll sign an autograph for you, too," I offer with a warm smile.

"Huh?" Georgia scoffs.

I hold out my hand. "Do you have a Sharpie? I left mine in my locker."

Georgia slides the papers into her notebook and stuffs them into her backpack. "I don't want an autograph from you, Lyric."

"Then...?" I question her, unsure of what's happening with her right now. "What's up?"

I'm not completely clear why my girl is acting so bizarre. I know she's used to me being there for her, but now it's my turn to bask in the attention from all my followers. Why can't she be okay with that? There's enough of me to go around. *Right?*

"I just want to know if you still plan on going to group therapy with me," Georgia asks. She pinches her lips and exhales frustration. "The other day, you said you were going to hang with me at my appointment, then help Twinkie practice in your backyard again."

I whisper-ask, "Oh. Yeah. Well, when is your appointment?"

"It's next Thursday. After school."

"Yeah. I mean"—I turn to face her, noticing that she's down, sad even—"that's more than a whole week away. I don't see why not. I mean...I'm definitely going to do my best."

"See," Twinkie says. "We'll both be right by your side. You're not alone in any of this scary new stuff you're doing. And Lyric is still the same supportive friend she's always been."

"K. Cool." Georgia looks at me long enough for it to be awkward. Then she just shakes her head and walks away.

"Farealz. What's her deal?" I ask Twinkie, even though I'm more focused on waving at all the kids at the café tables who are trying to get my attention. I reach for Twinkie's hand to walk into all the excitement. "Why can't she just be happy for me?"

"She's just...scared," Twinkie says, grabbing my hand.

"Of what?"

Twinkie's head twists around to watch Georgia walk down the hall toward the courtyard. Alone.

I squeeze her hand before heading over to a table of kids waving me over. They hold up their phones to take pics with me. That's when I catch Twinkie gazing at the back of Georgia's cowboy hat. I hand her my phone to take pics of me posing with my fans and let her know, "I'm sure it's nothing."

When I'm out of sight, I'm forced to face my deflated feelings that are now screaming at me. I'm like oatmeal. At first, I'm good, firm and solid. But then, just the thought of being without Mom and Dad at home makes my head and my heart turn to mush. It's the weirdest thing. I can be so up one minute at school with all the cool stuff happening—and then, BOOM! My soul just crashes into my suede booties, and this heavy, sad feeling stomps all over it. I'm flip-flopping back to really low lows as I take the long way home after school. I'm dreading every step that takes me closer to the reality that they've left me again. I walk up to the front door after doing everything in my power to avoid opening it.

When I finally turn the key and walk inside, it's all dark. In the winter, the sun sets in the middle of the afternoon, and by the time I get home, it's pitch-black. Today is no different. And since Mom and Dad are on the road somewhere in Barcelona, the house is eerily silent, except for the TV noise buzzing from Aunt Jackie's room. You'd think I'd be used to this since they've been touring for years, but it never gets easier. I just wish Mom and Dad were here. I just wish they were normal parents. You know, the kind who have dinner with their kids every night, even if it's takeout. Or the kind who tuck their kids into bed and talk about all the things they're grateful for before lights out. My Aunt Jackie is always here, but she's usually snoring in her room to *Murder, She Wrote*. Don't get me wrong, I love that old lady, but it's def *nawt* the same as Jade Darby. Not the same as Mom.

I walk through the living room and flip the light on

in the kitchen. Dinner is one of my least favorite times of day, mainly because I've gotten so used to eating alone. That's not something I'd wish on my internet trolls, not even on Stormy Jackson. I sigh and open the refrigerator. It's pretty empty, short of a few apples that are starting to get mushy and a container of spring-mix lettuce that's wilting and making the fridge stink.

I open my delivery apps, order a veggie pizza from Fat Sal's, and trudge upstairs with a bag of Spicy Sweet Chili Doritos wrapped in my arms. I snuggle the bag and head to my room to watch old episodes of *American Rockstar.* It's the one thing that will keep me distracted from feeling alone. And sad.

CHAPTER 16

I cried myself to sleep last night. Then when my alarm clock went off, I cried a little bit more. *I can't people today,* I admitted to myself, and rolled over in bed. It was like that the next day, too, and the one after that. I told Aunt Jackie I had the flu, but the truth is the deep sadness that had crept in was far worse than a fever and the sniffles. And no matter how hard I tried, I couldn't get back to that on-top-of-the-world feeling. I knew Mom and Dad loved me; I just couldn't shake the thought of not being important to them. At least not important enough to be here for me and not on the road in front of all those strangers.

Their fans. I guess I should understand because the funny thing is that my followers were the ones who kept me going when I was all alone. But I don't understand. I'm Jade Darby's daughter. Still, I read and reread the comments under the *American Rockstar* posts of my audition video. If I'm being honest, I did feel seen. And special. So bizarre that strangers can have that effect.

A whole week goes by before I'm able to respond to texts. Twinkie texted that Stormy Jackson stood in for me as Dorothy when I didn't make it to rehearsal last weekend.

AND she was really good

AND u have a responsibility 2 all ur fans

AND you promised G. Therapy buddies

2day

ANDDDDD ur Instafamous!!!!!!!!!!!!!!!!!!

Thank gawd for fame and followers; they turned out to be the perfect distraction from my feelings. Because at the end of the day, Twinkie was right and I didn't want to lose my fans. Or my Instafame. The thought of it pulled me out from under the covers.

U up?

I finally text back a thumbs-up emoji.

I'm up, but the silence in the house is deafening.

I hate mornings when Mom isn't here. I know she's not the best cook in the world, or even in our house, for that matter, but there's something about seeing Jade Darby in the kitchen with a spatula in her hand whipping up burned chocolate-chip pancakes that makes me feel, well, loved. I'd never admit this to her, but I also feel loved when she's fussing at me after I've done something that disappoints her—like forging her signature on the *American Rockstar* consent form.

The house smells different, too, when she's not here. There's just the aroma of Aunt Jackie's morning farts, and they like to linger in the air. My phone dings again, and it's the text that gets me going.

Good. Now check ur #s.

I check my Insta numbers and see that my following has hit a whopping 25,479. My video has been viewed tons of times, too. My thoughts start to race, and I can't stop thinking about Mom not being by my side for this wild ride. Then all the "what ifs" start to take over and fly through my brain.

What if she doesn't let me compete on the show?

What if she keeps touring and I have to finish this adventure alone?

What if she's so disappointed in me that she stops talking to me?

What if she records a new album and isn't around... ever?

What if she never lets me chase my dreams?

When I can't slow down my thoughts, I slide to the floor and cross my legs, my hands settling on my knees. Dad taught me how to meditate last year when I was having nightmares. I've been trying to do it more, but lately, I haven't been as committed as I should. The way I figure, though, is there's no better time than now, especially with the pressure on me to live up to my new image. Everybody expects me to be big. Even me. But I guess that's the price of fame.

I close my eyes and manage to sit still for about twenty seconds until my thoughts take over and all I can think about is the fact that I now have over TWENTY-FIVE THOUSAND followers. I open my left eye and peek at my phone that's a few inches from my knee. I reach for it and slide it closer with my pinky. Then I just throw the whole meditation sesh away and focus on my numbers. I blink a few times to make sure I'm reading it right.

26,200 followers. Whoa! Almost seven hundred more in just a few HOURS!!

There's no way I can stop the racing thoughts now that it's all actually happening. I'm blowing up! So instead of self-care, I opt for a cinnamon raisin bagel with vegan cream cheese that I end up tossing into the trash. Still no appetite. But I manage to force a shower and order an Uber for a quick Starbucks run. Normally, I'd hop on my bike, but now that I'm Instafamous, I can't be caught scooting around town on two wheels.

My phone dings and then it dings again.

I check the message and see that it's Twinkie confirming our practice sesh after school:

> THX 4 HELPING ME B4
>
> R WE ON 4 2DAY AFTER SCHL?
>
> OPERATION HELPING TWINKIE—
>
> TAKE 2?
>
> XO

I almost forgot that I promised her I'd make time to go over her lines and her songs again. The way I see it, she's already the perfect Lion. It's funny how other people see us clearly but we're the ones who struggle to see our true selves.

When I arrive at school, I'm ready for my close-up. Twinkie was right; I have a responsibility to my fans to be the Instastar they want! More access to my superstar life for my socials! *I enlisted the perfect director, Stella Rose!* I think as I sip my venti caramel macchiato and pose for her. I stick out my leg with the faux leather fringes down the side and shake it out so they dance in the wind.

"OMG! You look fab!" Stella Rose says as I walk up the front steps of Valentine Middle. "And the lighting is killer." She steadies the camera and cues the two twin boys holding a bounce board that looks like a plate of aluminum foil. A boom mic that the short boy is struggling to hold over my head is pointed at my mouth.

"I need just one shot of you walking up the stairs for the reel."

"Where'd you get the twins?" I ask Stella Rose as she stares into her camera lens.

"Audiovisual club," she answers like it's perfectly normal for twin boys to be part of my camera crew in front of the school on a random Thursday. "And…action!" she yells like we're on a studio lot.

The other kids move aside and watch as I waltz down the block and up the school steps. "Cut!" Stella Rose yells when Stormy and Buster interrupt our flow and barge straight into the shot. Stormy waits for my eyeballs to find hers, and then she snarls at me.

"You're really doing the most," she says, sucking her teeth and shaking her head in what looks like disappointment. My retaliation is a frosty eye roll followed by the biggest fluff of my barrel curls. *Humph.* What does she know? She's not on her way to being a contestant on the world's biggest stage.

"Let's go again," Stella Rose directs as I hit my mark in the middle of the block beside the fire hydrant. She yells, "So glad you're back. You were definitely missed."

I smize with my eyes when she yells, "And action!"

I strut my stuff, connecting with the crowd of admirers, making sure to wave so I seem relatable. I blow a kiss at Winnie, who's waiting for the HoneyBee cheerleaders to get out of her way. It's at this point that I push the fame thing too far. I'm pretty sure she rolls her eyes at me. But I shrug it off and pretend it never happened as soon as Stella Rose yells, "Cut! That was purrrfection."

"Did you get what you needed?" I ask, motioning for

one of the twins to pass me my coffee. I check my Insta and see that I've gained another few hundred followers since Stella Rose posted our latest reel.

Stella Rose checks the footage and then grins. "With you as my subject, it's always easy peasy."

"Lemon squeezy," I finish, high-fiving her as we walk into the school building with the rest of the crew behind us. As soon as we get inside, they make haste setting up the next shot.

"Now I need to get you walking down the hall. It's, like, expected," she says, swinging her arm in the air, motioning to the crew that it's go time.

"Just be you," she says, admiring me. "You were born for this."

She doesn't have to tell me twice. I adjust my blingy sunnies and grip my coffee cup, swishing my hips down the hall. Out of my periphery, I can see Stella Rose recording my every move. One by one, kids join in on the hype and follow us down the hall, and I think to myself that I'm a natural at being important.

By the time I get to my locker, I'm surrounded by mostly sixth graders and a handful of seventh graders. And then there's Twinkie and Georgia.

"And... cut!" Stella Rose yells into the crowd, her voice bouncing off the walls in the hall.

“What do you think you’re doing?” Georgia challenges as she and Twinkie confront me. “What is all the commotion about?”

Twinkie’s eyes dart back and forth between me and the crowd, trying to make sense of it all. “It looks like you have an entourage.”

“I thought Twink was your manager. Did you run any of this by her?”

“She’s not my actual manager, G,” I explain. “That’s just for play. Look.” I spin around on my heels, pointing to the sound guy, the lighting kid, and my acclaimed director. “Stella Rose actually won honorable mention in a documentary contest.”

“What’s that got to do with Twinkie? She’s been holding you down since this thing started with you and *Rockstar*.”

“Yeah. Yeah. But she’s not an award-winning doc producer. She’s just…”

Georgia grabs her cowboy hat and yanks it off her head. “Just what?”

Twinkie is twirling her pendant necklace around her index finger, her ponytail ping-ponging between Stella Rose and me. I really didn’t mean for a whole confrontation to go down in the hallway outside of homeroom. But, alas, here we are.

"Nothing," I say, sipping my macchiato. Then I tell her what Dad always says. "You're making a mountain of a molehill, Georgia."

"Dude! What does that even mean?!" she spouts, waving her hat around in the air. I watch her grab Twinkie's hand and pull her away. As they head for homeroom, she turns back to check out all the kids pointing their camera phones at me. "And since you're blowing off your peeps, I guess I shouldn't count on you to be there for me after school either. You'll be filming with your fans, I'm sure."

"What are we doing after school?" I ask, completely stumped.

Twinkie's face smushes into a frown. "Are you serious? It's only Georgia's big day; her first group therapy session. After that, you promised to help me with my songs and stuff for the play." She looks at me, but it feels like she's looking right through me, and I start to feel small.

Twinkie's eyes narrow, and her voice softens. "Did you really forget?"

"Of course not," I fumble. "I got your texts."

"You had to remind her via text?" Georgia snips, then turns to me. "And you still forgot?!" She beats her toe against the floor before she barks, "You know what... never mind!"

"It was a brain fart," I try to explain as the bell rings.

But she leaves as all the other kids scatter, filing into classrooms to start their day. But not my crew. Instead, we dip into the bathrooms to hide. When the final bell rings, one of the twins pokes his head into the hallway to check for grownups. And when it is clear, he whistles for everyone to rally.

I don't usually condone skipping class, but this is an urgent matter. Stella Rose and the twins sneak into the theater to grab more footage. This time, we get quick shots of me singing on stage for the next reel. Fun fact: If I'm going to get my Insta count to hit a gazillion in three days, then I'm going to need to feed the beast.

Stella Rose positions her camera in front of me to catch my vibe. "Now, sing a few notes from your big song." She looks at me over her tortoise glasses and grins. "It's my fave song, B-T-dubs."

"Mine and Jade's, too," I say, hoping these videos show my mom that I'm ready.

I turn my back to the camera, and when Stella Rose yells, "Action!" I ease toward the camera, staring into the lens like it leads to all my hopes and dreams, because, well, it does.

I'm singing a capella, pulling emotion from deep inside of me, and just when I'm about to hit my first big note, the door swings open. I gulp when Principal Pootie storms into the theater.

"What are you all doing in here?" he demands to know.

Stella Rose cowers behind me, and I try to explain, even though I know we're in deep. "Just, uh, getting a few reels done, for uh..."

"Lyric Darby! This is grounds for detention. You're supposed to be in class."

"Yeah, I know. But we needed to get a few more shots for—"

"I don't care what you're working on. This is class time."

I grab my backpack from the wings and head down the stage steps, up the aisle, and out the door. "On my way," I say before he has a chance to dish out demerits.

"I'll meet you at lunch," Stella Rose says, inching past Pootie and the twins. But before she can squeeze out the door, he takes her really expensive camera and holds it high above his head.

"I'll keep this until after school, thank you very much."

"But... but—"

"Unless you'd like to pick it up at detention."

"Nope. We're good," I say, grabbing Stella Rose by the elbow and pulling her down the hall with me. At this point, detention means death. How am I supposed to enjoy being Instafamous if I'm dead?

The rest of the school day was an absolute whirlwind. I didn't know being a star would be so exhausting. When my Insta hit 27,200 followers, almost all of the sixth graders lined up to take a picture with me and post to their socials. It feels like I'm always racing to get to class after posing with so many of my fans.

"Hey, Lyric!" the reporter from the school newspaper yells at me after school. I prance toward him, with Stella Rose and the twins behind me. I can feel Stella Rose motioning for the twins to get in position as she frames the perfect shot of me.

Wearing a welcome smile for the reporter, I tap my spiked heels on the tiled floor. "What's good?" I ask, fist-bumping him into a hand explosion. Mom always says it's important to make nice with the media.

"You have any interest in an interview? I'm on a tight deadline, but with your sudden stardom on the internet and at school, I didn't want to miss an opportunity to give you face time in the paper."

"Well, that's really kind of you," I gush to him as I walk toward the exit sign over the front door. I peek outside and see Georgia and Twinkie waiting for me at the bottom of the steps. Twinkie leans on the banister and checks her watch.

"Of course you can have an interview." I turn to Stella Rose and smile into her camera. "Anytime."

"Great," he says, his eyes sparkling. "How about now?"

"Oh, I uh..." I push the door open and glimpse Georgia huffing and puffing, pacing the sidewalk in front of Twinkie. If I don't hurry, she's going to be late for her group therapy session. "Does it have to be right now?"

"Yeah, it does. I have a tight deadline. It just doesn't feel like this edition will be complete without our rising star in it."

I turn away from the camera and whisper-ask, "Will I get the front page?"

The reporter's face crinkles into a wide smile. "Of course. You're all everybody's talking about at Valentine Middle."

I bite the inside of my cheek and think. Then I make the big decision to ignore the good angel sitting on my left shoulder. Georgia doesn't really need me anyway. "Okay," I say to the reporter. "Let's do it."

"Great," he says, leading me down the hallway, toward the conference room where all the important school business is handled. Stella Rose and the twins scramble to keep up with us.

"Just keep recording," Stella Rose says to the twin with the boom mic. I can tell that his arms are starting to burn when he almost smashes the microphone into my forehead.

Honestly, I really did plan on going to the group therapy session with Georgia and then spending the evening singing with Twinkie on my backyard stage. But I'm not sure what I'm supposed to do now that I'll be the lead story in the *Valentine Middle Gazette*. It's all happening so fast. If Georgia or Twinkie had a glow-up this epic, I'd be supportive of them.

I sit in the seat at the middle of the conference room table and wait for the reporter to start the interview. "We need just another half hour to finish getting everything set up. We want to take some photos to go along with the piece."

"How long after that?"

"Shouldn't take more than two or three hours to get everything done."

A few hours?!

"It's last-minute, so I had to call the photographer and get this added to his schedule. He was doing yearbook stuff, but he said he'd stop cuz you're worth it." The reporter pats me on my shoulder. "He's so good; your shots are guaranteed to look amazing."

I guess that's okay.

When my phone dings, the hairs on the back of my neck stand. I know it's Georgia and Twinkie. There's no need to even check. I shove my phone into my messenger bag. It's better if I don't engage. I have to be on point for my fans; my answers to these questions will matter to all the other aspiring superstars at school. After all, they need me; I'll just have to deal with my squad later.

"How do you feel?" Stella Rose asks as the reporter gets ready to press RECORD on his phone.

"Incredible," I admit, ignoring the guilty vibes that are flittering around my head and landing right over my heart.

CHAPTER 17

The next day at school, Georgia and Twinkie barely say two words to me. I can tell Twinkie wants to talk, but every time I corner her, Georgia snatches her away.

"Hey, Twink. Are you ready for rehearsal today?" I ask her between classes at our lockers. Georgia stayed behind in Mr. Chang's, so I took the opportunity to check in and try to smooth the bumpy waters.

Twinkie shrugs. She's standing on her tiptoes, digging out her science book when she coolly says, "It's Friday. Where else would I be?"

"I see. Well, we can walk over to the theater together if you want."

When Twinkie doesn't respond with her usual chipper smile, I press harder. "Look. Are you mad at me or something?" I lean against my locker, not taking my eyes off her. "Seriously, Twink, what's the deal?"

"Um. Well. No." She puts the book in her backpack and reaches for her gym shorts. Then she stops. "Actually...yes! You weren't there for me or Georgia. And...and we needed you. We're going through stuff, too, Lyric."

"What are you talking about?" My arms squirm around my torso as I try to come up with a reason—any reason—for ditching them yesterday. But before I can tell another lie, Georgia barges into our conversation and takes over.

"If you can't figure it out, then you have bigger problems besides dissing your girls."

"I didn't diss you," I fume back at Georgia. "And who says *diss* anymore anyway?"

"See, that's the exact problem," Georgia retorts, snatching the toothpick out of her mouth. "You care about all the wrong things."

I watch her walk away, her fingers wrapped around

Twinkie's wrist. This isn't good. We've been friends since the first day of forever, and I've never been on the receiving end of their disappointment. I open my locker and grab my science book, feeling all the feels. But I still believe I can fix it. Once I'm plucked out of obscurity and shining brilliantly on *American Rockstar*, everyone will understand. Even Jade Darby.

"Hey, Lyric," a tall, lanky boy with French braids calls to me from down the hall. "Hold up a second," he says, jogging my way. I decide to wait for him instead of chasing behind Georgia. She needs time to cool off anyway.

"What's up?" I ask as he catches his breath. I recognize him from the basketball team. He's one of the eighth graders that the girls go gaga over.

"I'm Zain, and I'm the new president of the film club." He holds out his hand for me to shake.

I can see why they're smitten with him. I shrug, offer him my fingers, and grin. "Hey, Zain. What's good?"

"Well, some of the officers were talking about you last night on our group text, and we wanted to know if we could profile you for the school website?"

"What exactly does that mean?" I ask, even though I already know the answer is going to be a resounding *YES*. That one time when "Paper Cuts" got trashed on a big blog, I didn't get why Mom didn't cry. That's when she explained to me that all publicity is good publicity. She never cared about the trolls, even when they dragged her name through the internet mud.

"Principal Pootie asked us to put a short piece together for the spring semester updates. We think featuring you would be pretty cool."

"I'm into that," I say, thinking of all the potential followers.

"I can send you the questions ahead of time so you're ready. We want to shoot today after school."

Ugh! Fridays are for rehearsal. But then again... publicity. "I'm here for it."

"I know you're in the play and practice is today, so I'm not sure if that works for you."

"Oh," I start, without thinking. "Don't worry about the play. It's amateurish anyway."

"OMG!" a voice shrills from behind me. "You're a total fraud. I knew it! Don't you know that Dorothy is the role of a lifetime?"

I crane my neck to see Stormy Jackson stalking past. "And nothing about our dear Dorothy is amateurish; she's a kind, generous, loving character."

"Welll," I whisper-explain to her. "Actually... Dorothy killed a total stranger within the first five minutes of the play. So technically, she's a murderer."

Stormy's eyes bug out of her head, and her whole body starts to shake. "Dorothy is a musical theater icon. A true gift to the thespian community." I watch as Stormy's eyes start to water. She balls her fists and yells at me. "You don't deserve us! You never did!"

"Don't pay her any mind," I say to Zain, who looks so uncomfortable that I think he's about to cancel our meetup. I watch him take a giant step backward.

"Email me the questions and I'll be ready after school. It's cool," I say, doing my best to distract him from the drama.

"But what about Dorothy and the play?" he asks as I lead him in the opposite direction of Stormy.

"They'll understand."

After school, I finish up with Zain and head to play rehearsal. *I'm only forty-five minutes late, so it shouldn't be a big deal,* I'm thinking to myself as I open the door to the theater. I hadn't planned on being more than fifteen minutes late, but the interview was so exciting that I lost track of time. It's hard walking in the opposite direction when all the attention is on me. I hadn't banked on this part of the Instafame game, but it's not easy to turn away when one second you're a nobody, and then… POOF! You're the new IT GIRL. Being liked and feeling important is kind of addictive, like those caramel macchiatos with extra whipped cream. Confession: Yes, I can completely feel it in my gut; I'm taking this whole thing way too far. But I'm becoming my favorite subject.

"Hey! You're late," Stella Rose says as I walk over to her seat at the end of the aisle. "We told everyone you were going live over a half hour ago." She holds up her phone and points it at me, counting down from five, four, three, two...

Stella Rose came up with the idea to go live at rehearsal. At this point, I have all the followers I need to be eligible to compete in *American Rockstar*, but I might as well do everything in my power to secure my spot on the show. Stella Rose is a marketing genius, I have to admit. Recording me in rehearsal should be just the thing to push me over the edge, grab a few thousand more followers, and wow all my new fans. Who doesn't love a behind-the-scenes moment? With me onstage prepping and performing, the producers and judges will see just how much they need me on their show. Let's face it, I'm what's hot right now.

"Yes, Stella Rose, I was born ready!" I smile into the camera phone as Twinkie completely destroys the opening to her big song, "Mean Ole Lion." Oh no. I watch her onstage, forgetting all the words, her cheeks turning very deep shades of Corvette red. I thought she practiced yesterday after Georgia's therapy session. Why does she sound like she's never even heard the song before?

"Ooh, is that her voice or is someone strangling her to death?" Buster jokes from downstage.

When all the kids laugh at the venom he's still spewing at Twinkie, I see her courage start to walk right off that stage, up the aisle, and out the door. The kids onstage muffle their ears, some shaking their heads, mouthing a muted but very loud *NOOO.*

"Saanvi!" Ms. Pepper yells over Twinkie's shrilly voice. She's sitting at the piano, pinching her brows. "Remember to stay on key. And your pitch. You have to watch your pitch, dear."

"Her pitch?" Buster yells over Twinkie's sad voice. "Just strike her out already!"

Magic and LuLu try to shush some of their fellow Munchkins in the audience who are laughing so hard that they are doubled over, gripping their bellies. But Georgia takes a completely different approach. Faster than Twinkie can sing the next stanza, Georgia swipes her leg under Buster's and takes him out. All we hear is a loud *SPLAT!* The next thing we see is Buster on the floor searching for the culprit. Georgia was so quick with the takedown that he never saw it coming.

"Stop! Stop!" Mr. Reynolds barks from in front of the stage. "Everybody...everything...everywhere...just stop!"

A wave of giggles crashes against the stage, and Twinkie flies into the wings. "I quit!" she announces. "I can't do this!" we hear her say from backstage.

Mr. Reynolds moves to follow her, but it's too late. He turns to quiet the kids in the audience but stops when he sees both of Georgia's parents.

What are they doing here? I ask myself, rewinding our last few conversations in my head. They were pretty short, but I'm certain there was never any talk about her parentals coming to watch her practice.

I watch them both storm down the aisle toward their daughter.

"Come down here right now," Georgia's dad orders, motioning for her with his index finger.

"Mr. and Mrs. Reign, uh, hi," Mr. Reynolds greets them, frazzled and disturbingly sweaty. The look on his face says that he's completely clueless and has no idea why they're here either. "Um. To what do we owe this surprise visit?" he sputters.

"Georgia knows exactly why we're here," Mrs. Reign says, watching Georgia ease on down the stage. "Don't you, Georgia?"

"What's happening right now?" Stella Rose asks,

poking her head from behind her camera phone. "Everything is falling apart."

I whisper-shrug, "I don't know."

Georgia grabs her backpack from her seat, never saying a word. But Buster giggles from stage left, and we all hear him, even Georgia's mom, who huffs loud enough to shut him up.

"We had an agreement," she fusses at her daughter.

"What happened?" I ask Twinkie as she gathers her stuff from her seat and follows behind Georgia.

"You would know that she didn't go to therapy yesterday if you would've shown up for her," Twinkie says to me. "And for me."

I try to stop Twinkie, but she's over it all. "So she's out? That's it?"

"We both are!"

"And so are you!" I feel someone poking me in the shoulder. I spin around to see Stormy Jackson wearing a devilish grin. "*I'm* the new Dorothy."

Mr. Reynolds eyes me from in front of the stage and announces, "Lyric. So nice of you to join us."

"I, uh… I was, uh…"

"This is becoming a pattern, Lyric. You keep showing up late and making the cast and crew wait for you."

"I had a thing that I needed to handle," I sort of lie.

"Your uncle . . . or your aunt—or was it your grandmother this time?" Buster makes me his new target. "How many family members do you have in crisis?"

"I'm really sorry," I admit, trying to keep my head above water. I try not to go under, but I'm on the verge of drowning. "The time. It just got away from me."

Mr. Reynolds takes a deep breath and loosens his tie. Before he can say another word, he unbuttons his top button and bends over. I think he's going to pass out, but then he stands and announces to everyone in the theater, "This is a big commitment. We depend on each other. We are a family creating something very special on a very tight timeline. You need to be punctual, and you need to know your lines and songs. That goes for everyone."

"I don't know if you know, Mr. Reynolds, but I'm auditioning for *American Rockstar*," I peep, trying to salvage my entire career. "I already advanced to round three. They want me."

"Well, since that's your priority right now, Lyric, Stormy will take over your role as Dorothy. Like I've already said, the cast needs commitment; they're depending on it. I'm sorry, but we do wish you the best of luck with the singing competition."

"So I'm not Dorothy anymore? I'm out of the play?"

"Yeah," Stormy says, pushing past me. "We're too amateurish for you anyway. Remember?"

"Ohmahgawsh!" Stella Rose screeches, staring at her phone.

"No?!" I protest, watching her hand as it starts to shake.

"Yes." Her eyes dart around the room, searching for answers. "I'm so sorry, Lyric. I don't know how this happened."

We both glare at her phone.

"This thing is still on," she cries, shutting off her phone.

"It was recording me that whole time? Recording me getting kicked out of the play? *My* play?" I feel tears sting my eyes. "Stella Rose, are you saying I was LIVE?"

I fall into a chair and palm my forehead.

Welp, now I'm definitely dead.

CHAPTER 18

The next morning, I wake up and flip-flop my arm around my bed, searching for my phone. *I know it's here somewhere,* I think to myself as I grasp at air between the comforter and the sheet.

Found it!

I also find the latest when I check my Insta.

My Live went viral.

And yes, with thousands of followers, I knew it was bound to happen. But it still reeks like old boiled eggs. Now the whole world has seen me get kicked out of the play like those same boiled eggs. *Ew!*

I peer my eyes halfway open and immediately text Twinkie.

Wut time r u going w me 2day?

I can't let a little viral moment (okay, a mega-viral moment) stop me from taking what's mine. I hope Bailey hasn't seen my feed. I desperately need my Twinkie. Even though I know she's probs still mad at me for ghosting my girls, I'm hoping we can just sweep it under the rug. Besides, she knows how important today is for me. Georgia might be deep in her feelings and not interested in showing up for me, but Twinkie is different.

I check my phone.

No response.

I check it five minutes later.

Still . . . no response.

I wriggle around in the bed and finally sit up, swinging my legs around to the floor. Georgia is usually the stubborn one; why is Twinkie picking up her annoying traits?

Focusing on my *Rockstar* outfit is easier, less annoying than trying to get inside my friend's twelve-year-old mind. I walk into my closet and survey the rows of fashion. I want my vibe to scream fierce and fabulous, but with a relatable touch. Everyone at the audition won't know that

I'm a star... at least not yet. So I need to walk in like the stage is my second home and I'm ready to own it.

Twinkie still hasn't texted back.

This is it, I think, pulling out my pink faux-leather vest—the one with the hanging tassels, braided fringes, and rhinestones down the sides. With my fishnets under my boyfriend jeans with the holes at the knees, it'll be vibes all day. I grab them from the denim shelf and hold them up to my waist. Then I remember the snake-buckle belt. A definite showstopper. Just like me.

I check my texts again to see if Twinkie is checking for me. Still nope. I know she sees me blowing her up.

I continue readying myself for auditions, trying to push the thought of Twink and Georgia as far away from my morning prep as possible. Instead, I focus on my song selection as I put the finishing touches on my hair.

I stop picking out my big spiral curls that are now framing my face perfectly and huff. Then I text:

> Sooooo I guess ur NAWT going 2 the
> pier w me?

I hit SEND and crawl past Aunt Jackie's room. When I get to the stairway, I fly downstairs for a few swigs of hot tea to awaken my voice. I check my texts again.

Nothing.

I just need to stay on track and prep. I gargle with a little salt water and open the front door, only to find Aunt Jackie knitting on the porch swing. I freeze, waiting for her to lecture me or fuss at me or...something. But all she says, never taking her eyes off her needles, is, "You know, being too full of yourself is a bit like trying to fit an elephant into a phone booth."

I know she's trying to get at something, so I ask, "Auntie, what's a phone booth?"

She loops her needle through the yarn, ignoring my question, and finishes. "It's a tight squeeze, and eventually, you'll have to let some of that hot air out!"

I check the time on my phone and try to hurry this along. "Auntie, what are you getting at?"

She swings a little and tries a different approach. "It's like trying to teach a goldfish to ride a bicycle. Now that's a real fishy situation."

I stand at the top step, waiting for her to explain herself, but instead, she bobs her head and smiles at her ball of yarn like she's said just enough.

I'm running out of time, so I barrel down the stairs toward my bike. That's when I hear her announce into the air, "You might want to leave the fish alone and pedal your way back to kindness. It'll save you and those cute little goldfish every time."

"Okay, Auntie. Whatever you say." I toss my hand in the air to wave, never looking back. Now I'm thinking about elephants and goldfish and all their animal cracker friends and wondering what they have to do with *American Rockstar.*

When I get to the curb, I shake out my curls and refocus. I text Twinkie to say:

> I guess ur mad at me but I was
> expecting u 2 b over it by now. I need
> u to b by my side 2day like u always r.
> This is annoying.

When I get to the Pier, there's a small line of people outside of the tents in the parking lot. It's a gloomy day, which happens more often than I like during this time of year.

Finally, I think when I see the three dots next to Twinkie's name alerting me that she's writing something back.

> TWINKIE: . . .

She's probably about to tell me she's on her way. I knew I could count on her. So good that Georgia didn't get in her head. Twinkie is my special girl. Unlike Georgia, who's always in her feelings, I can depend on Twinkie to hold me down.

I hop on my bike and glance at my phone, trying not to ride right into a tree. But then I notice that the three dots have disappeared.

Ugh! She deleted her text before she sent it to me. I legit HATE when that happens. Just say what you were about to say. *I'm not a mind reader, Twink!*

I race through Saturday traffic on Ocean Avenue, then round the corner to Starbucks on the Promenade and grab my preorder: a simple hot tea to coat my throat. When I get to the Pier, I walk my bike down to the production village in the massive parking lot and head toward the tents. That's when I spy Bailey. I try to get her attention, but I'm immediately shuffled into a whirlwind of organized chaos. One producer grabs me and takes a snapshot of my school ID, another slaps a cut-out piece of paper with the number three over my vest, and then another stands me in line for the stage. And just like that, I'm third to audition.

THIRD!

In front of me is a girl with long black hair that almost

touches her ankles. She's motioning to the producers, not uttering a peep. I know that move; she's saving her voice. I guess I'm doing the same since my support squad isn't here to listen to my nervous system kick into high gear and ramble on about Jade Darby, my destiny, or how long I've waited to be in front of the iconic judges, especially Girl Power.

That's when I see them.

Girl Power struts onto the stage and heads for the long table with the white tablecloth covering it. Gliding on air, they move to the cushy chairs, in front of the cameras. I can't stop staring. Every single one of my friends adores them. But I'm certain I love them the most.

I gawk at all three of them, not caring as much about the other two judges, who move to their seats with their hair and makeup girls perfecting their looks, too.

My armpits are wet. My palms are sticky. My knees are buckling. But I'm more ready than I've ever been—except for that one little disqualifying deet: I'm no longer Dorothy. But my big voice should make up for that. At least that's what I keep telling myself.

I look around at all the fuss being made over the judges. I was born for this life, to have my name in lights, to one day sit in those chairs. I'm praying Dorothy doesn't take it away.

"You're up third, Darby," a producer with chunky highlights says to me, squaring my shoulders. She talks into a microphone that's positioned over her head and then directs me. "When you step onstage, you'll have five seconds before you need to walk out to that little X in the middle of the stage."

I nod, making sure to take in every word he says. I can't mess this up. I've waited too long to get here. I know Mom and Dad will be proud once I'm booked on the show. I'm their legacy, after all. In a matter of minutes, after the two contestants in front of me audition, my entire life will change. This is gargantuan, I think, inhaling determination.

"Hey, kid!" Bailey greets me over the muffled noise from all the wannabe superstars waiting their turn behind me. Her eyes are warm. That's a good sign.

"Hey, Bailey!" If I act normal, maybe she won't bring up the fact that my Live went viral. Or that I got canned from the show. Or that I don't have performing arts or industry experience anymore. So normal it is.

I smile and continue, "I saw you earlier and tried to get your attention."

Then her speckled greenish-brown eyeballs turn to pity. I'd know those eyes anywhere. Every time Mom and Dad go out of town, it's exactly how my Aunt Jackie looks at me when they pull out of the driveway. Aunt Jackie never said she felt sorry for me because my parentals were always on the road, but she didn't need to because her sad eyes said it for her.

"I'm ready for my close-up," I say to her, trying to shift the mood back to normal.

"Uh, yeah. About that..."

"What's up, buttercup?" I ask, shrugging my shoulders.

I can feel my phone buzzing in the back pocket of my jeans. I grab it and let out a ghastly sigh. It's Mom. After reading her text, I'm pretty sure she's not happy either.

MOM: YOUR FATHER AND I ARE ON
OUR WAY HOME.

Now, whenever Mom uses all caps, she means serious business. The last time she sent me one of these capped-out texts, she told me I couldn't sing background at her holiday shows at the Grove because I had ditched school to watch her tech rehearsal. It was my first big singing gig. The stage positioned right in front of the twelve-foot Christmas tree. Next to the railroad tracks and the fountains that have music playing to the water gymnastics. In the center of it all!

I. Was. Devastated.

MOM: WE NEED TO TALK.

Now it's Christmas Show Canceled all over again.

I'm squeezing the phone so tightly that I might choke it to death when I feel my fingers buzzing again. I look down to see her next message.

MOM: I'M DISAPPOINTED IN YOU.

"Uh, Lyric," I hear Bailey say over my shoulder, her words now matching her eyes, dripping with pity. "We need to talk."

That's the last thing I want to do. I just want to sing.

I follow Bailey as she pulls me out of line and leads me behind one of the registration tents.

"What's going on?" I whisper-ask, silently begging the universe to fix this. "Is something wrong?"

"Yes," she says, getting straight to the point. Then she just stands there watching me, sort of how Principal Pootie does whenever he's waiting for us to announce why we've been called into his office when we've done something detention-worthy. I take this as my cue to fess up, but only halfway because at this point, I don't actually know what she knows.

"If you follow me on my socials, I can explain."

"I do. After posting you on *American Rockstar*'s Insta, I had to follow you. It would be career suicide not to follow you. You know, in case something devastating gets posted that could hurt the show."

"And about that, Bailey. I really appreciate you gifting me with all that amazing exposure and visibility. I've really been able to get my following up because of that—just like you asked."

"Well, unfortunately, your following isn't the primary issue anymore, Lyric."

I hope someone is saving my spot in line, I think.

"Now I'm *nawt* following," I lie, even though I'm completely following.

She crosses her arms over her chest and cuffs her biceps. "It's your Live, from yesterday, that's the issue."

I tap my press-on fingernails against my chin and pretend to think for a few seconds. In the distance, I can see the big stage with all the lights and mics surrounding the judges. What do I need to say to get on that stage?

Then I just blabber it all out, because at this point, I can't afford to waste any more time. I HAVE to get on that stage.

"Well... what had happened was—" I start.

"Lyric, you were fired from your play. And it went viral."

"Not *exactly* viral," I scoff.

Her brows dip into her head. "More than four thousand people saw it."

"Wow. That many, huh?" In my periphery, I see the first contestant step on stage.

"And action!" the director yells in the distance, cuing her big audition.

I have to get back in line, so I try to explain. "Bailey, don't you find it interesting that my fan base has quadrupled since we met? I think you and I have something special here. We make a good team, don't ya think?"

"Lyric, I think that all of this"—she points to the production team handling the lights, cameras, and all the action—"has gone to your head."

"I, uh"—I fidget with one of the faux-leather braids on my vest—"don't know what you mean." But I do. Twinkie and Georgia do, too.

"If what your play director said on your IG Live is true, then you've been letting your cast and crew down by being late and by not showing up. That's what I mean. Going to your head."

"I'm sorry, Bailey. It's just that I want this so bad, more than you'll ever understand. It's the only thing in my life that makes sense. When I'm on that stage, I feel like I matter, like I have purpose. Like I'm..." I swipe the tear that's crawling down my cheeks. "Like I'm...important."

Bailey digs into the pocket of her striped overalls and hands me a tattered napkin. "Here."

I take it and huff. "I'm not a bad person. I've just been in my mom's shadow all these years, trying to get her to see that I'm good at this thing, too. That I can be somebody, too."

"I'm sure Jade Darby doesn't expect you to be like her. I'm sure she expects you to be like you. And that's somebody, too. That's somebody really important—who matters."

"I dunno."

"Look, kid. I can't risk it and let you get on that stage in front of the judges."

"But—but..."

"I'd lose my job if I broke the rules. Besides, I'm not the only one following you on Insta, which means I'm not the only one who knows you're not qualified to compete on *American Rockstar* anymore." She puts her hands on my shoulders and sighs. "You need to have performing arts or industry experience. Your school musical was barely enough to clear you, if I'm being honest. But since you're Jade Darby's daughter, we looked the other way. But now—"

"Yeah." I dab my wet eyes with the napkin. "I know."

"And today, you don't even have that."

I stand behind the tent and kick my shoe into the cement, stubbing my toe. Somehow, I don't even feel the pain. My heart is broken, and that's the only pain that matters.

The edges of Bailey's lips curl into a half smile. "But."

"But what?"

"But. What if I told you I could hold your spot if I registered you as an alternate? They don't have to perform today to nab a final spot in the top sixty-four."

"I'll take it." Then I realize I have no idea what I'm getting into. "Wait. How does someone become an alternate? And what do they have to do once they become one? And if it means I can still compete, where do I sign up?"

"Slow down," she says, shaking her head. "Some contestants become alternates because they're sick, but we really liked their last two performances. Other times, a contestant might need to leave early because of an emergency, but we know they're special. It all depends. All kinds of things happen behind the scenes in show business, kid."

My eyes dart around the production village. When I hear the director yell, "Take five!" and then spy the judges walking by, I yell at Bailey.

"I'll take it!"

"Being an alternate doesn't guarantee you a spot."

"I know."

"You might not get to perform next week for the first live show either."

"I know."

"It's just a hold. If you want to be guaranteed a spot, you have to get that experience, and for you, that means being in your school play. I mean, as long as you're still Jade Darby's daughter."

"I am." I giggle, finally feeling relief. "I'll make it happen. Pinky swear."

"If you can't get back in your play, that slot will just go to the next alternate in line."

"I know. You can count on me." I reach up and throw my arms around her. "Bailey, thank you. Thank you so much."

"You're really good, Lyric. And I know this show could really use your talent." Bailey smiles at me again, but this time the pity is gone. "And even if you don't get a final spot for the live show in a few weeks, you still matter. Remember that. You may have messed up at school, but I still see something amazing in you." She rests her hands on my shoulders. "Your bravery, your heart, your determination. All that's pretty cool, kid."

I try really hard to see what she sees. But I don't. Right

now, I just see someone who almost had it all. Then poof! It went away.

But I'm determined to get it back.

I squeeze her even harder this time until I hear her back crack. "Sorry."

She takes my phone and plugs her number into it. "You know what you need to do. Here," she says, handing it back to me. "Let me know when it's done."

Bailey starts to walk away when we both hear someone call her name from inside the tent.

I roll on my tiptoes and yell after her, "I'll get my part back if it's the last thing I do."

CHAPTER 19

The ride home on my bike was a strange one. I stopped at the Cheesecake Factory to order a slice of coconut cream pie cheesecake and vibe with all the stuff that was swirling around my head—and in my heart. But it's just sitting on the table watching me watch it. So I text Twinkie to let her know that I didn't get to sing in front of Girl Power. At this point, I'm feeling all the feels. There's frustration and confusion hanging out, and then a few seconds later, gratitude and relief join my pity party when it dawns on me that Bailey didn't have to give me another shot at making the show. But she did.

I get the dessert to go and pay my tab. *This is my last chance to show that I'm truly an American Rockstar,* I'm thinking as I ride up Wilshire toward my house. I've done a lot of damage in the last few weeks, alienating my friends who have always been there for me. But now that no one is talking to me, how am I going to make things right?

"Don't tell Georgia I'm here," I hear Twinkie's voice say as I round the corner and walk up to my front door. She's kicking her feet around on the porch swing, staring at the leftover clouds in the sky.

I take a deep breath. "Hi."

"Hi."

We both look up to the heavens for a few awkward heartbeats.

"I got your text," she continues.

"Yeah?"

"Yeah."

I sit beside her on the swing.

We're quiet long enough to watch a butterfly flit around the entire rosebush before flying away.

"I know how much you were looking forward to today," she finally says, fiddling with her satin Valentine Middle jacket.

"I know I haven't been the friend you needed me to be,

Twinkie. I know I messed up. Like, really messed up. It's just that—"

"I quit the play," she interrupts me. I watch her study the elastic that's wrapped around her wrist. Then she picks a few lint balls from it.

"If I had anything to do with that, I'm really sorry. I know how big of a deal it was for you to get in front of all those people and audition."

"It wasn't about you. In the end, I let my fear get in the way of practicing. And I needed the practice. Like, a lot."

"I wasn't there to help you."

"No. You weren't."

"I'm really sor—"

"I shouldn't need you to help me practice. I had the music, I had the songs..."

"But you didn't have your friend who promised she'd be there—by your side."

Twinkie turns to me, her soft eyes checking me. "No. You weren't."

"Can I make it up to you?"

She places her hand on top of mine. "Can you make it up to yourself?"

I'm going to do my best.

The pounding in my chest slows to a soft thump. "Do

you think you have it in you to give me another chance? To be there for you?"

She smiles for the first time since we've been sitting on the swing sharing soul space.

I missed our special bond. "That would be a good first step in me making it up to myself," I say.

"I see."

"Because knowing that you're hurting hurts me, too."

She puts her hand on top of mine and sighs. "Of course. You're my friend."

"And I'll do better." I really will. "Can I tell you something big?"

She nods, and I take this as my cue to be brutally honest.

"I realized that I was doing to you exactly what my mom did to me. And you deserve better than that."

"We both do." And that's all she says before lifting her gaze back to the clouds.

I put my other hand on top of hers, and that same butterfly glides over and lands on top of her head.

Then we smile—until Mom's Range Rover screeches into the driveway and scares off the butterfly.

Aunt Jackie pokes her matted wig out the front door and warns, "Mom's home!"

"Uh-oh," I utter to Twinkie.

We look back and forth at each other, then at Mom as she gets out of the car and barrels toward us.

"This doesn't look good," Twinkie whisper-announces, and scoots out of the swing. She grabs her jelly-bean purse, blows me air kisses, and bolts out the front yard, yelling over her shoulder, "Hi, Mr. and Mrs. Darby!"

"Hello, Saanvi," Dad says to the back of her long ponytail as she motors down the block.

I turn to rush into the house, waving my hand in the air. "Uh, hi, Mom."

"Do you know how many times I've tried calling you?" she questions me. "Your father and I need answers."

"About what?" I try on fake confusion but she's not having it.

"Lyric Whitney Houston Darby!"

"Okay, but you weren't going to let me audition for *American Rockstar*." I dive right into it. "You said so yourself."

"Yes, but that doesn't mean you get to go do it anyway. I'm your mother, and what I say carries weight around here."

"But... you're never here," I mutter under my breath.

"Lyric, we talked about this. I'm working, and my work requires me to be on the road doing shows to get my music out there."

"So... why can't I do that, too?"

"Because."

"Because why?" I sigh. "Mom, don't you get it? I want to be just like you."

Mom freezes like she just spotted a stop sign.

"Baby, you're only twelve years old. You're still a kid, and I want you to have a kid's life, enjoy all the things a kid should enjoy." She pops her hip and sits into it. "I told you what your grandma did to me and how lonely it all was. Give it some time." She spins around to Dad. "Right, honey?"

"But, Mom. I'm ready now. I don't want to be in Chicago with a normal life. I want this. All of it."

Dad circles the island in the middle of the kitchen and grabs the half-eaten bag of kale chips from the uneven ceramic bowl I made in my pottery class last year. "Well, Jade. I don't know. Honestly. She's gotten herself all the way to the top sixty-four."

"And she did that without our consent."

Dad crunches on a big chip. "And that's saying a lot. Determination and talent. I don't know, honey."

"She lied to them about our consent. How did you do that? I know you needed our signature on some kind of release form."

I look at my fingernails and start to peel the press on right off.

"Well, I might have... Maybe I... If I recall, I uh..."

"She obviously signed your name, Jade," Dad recovers for me. "And if I remember correctly, when we were young, you did some unorthodox things, too, in order to make your dreams come true."

"But I was older than her, Elvis. Much older at that point."

Mom's eyes pinch, and I bet she wishes Dad was anywhere but here.

"Jade. Think about it. You were young once, too."

"Stop bringing that up, Elvis; we're not talking about me right now." She raps her fingernails over the stack of magazines on the island. "And I'm not twelve!"

Dad grabs her elbow and moves her to the kitchen table. He pulls out a chair and motions for her to sit. Then he sits down beside her. He looks between me and Mom and smiles.

"She's just like you, Jade Darby. She's always been just like you."

"I know. That's why I don't want her to go through all the mess I had to go through."

"But I think she's ready."

"I am ready," I say to them, taking a seat at the table, too. "Really. I am."

"And to be honest, I think she's been ready for a while."

"It can be a scary world out there, Lyric. And I just want to protect you."

"We'll be right by her side, every step of the way." Dad gets up to put his arms around Mom. "It won't be like it was with us. We only had each other." He kisses the back of Mom's hand. "Our superstar has the one and only Jade Darby by her side for this incredible ride."

Mom shakes her head and sighs. "I love you so much. I just want you to be prepared for this business."

"I know."

"I'm not trying to hold you back. I'm just…"

"Trying to protect me like you wish Grandma would've protected you," I finish for her.

"You're maturing right before my eyes," she says into a deep sigh. "The summer your grandmother moved us to LA, I was scheduled to attend scout camp in Indiana with my best friend, Jodie. We were going to be gone for two whole weeks. It was all we could talk about. All our friends were going, and we stayed up late at night coordinating outfits. It was going to be epic, especially since my birthday fell smack dab in the middle of camp. Jodie planned to have a pool party for all the girls in our troop, and we went shopping at the mall to find matching bathing suits. She was just as excited as I was. She even made arrangements for cupcakes and ice cream to be served back at the cabin. Neither one of us could barely sleep the week leading up to camp."

"I already know how this movie ends," I say, palming my face. "It's just sad at this point, Mom." I say to Dad, "Grandma was a beast."

"Jodie sent me pictures in the mail of all the girls blowing out candles on my chocolate cupcakes."

I gasp. "She never canceled the party?"

"Jodie was one of those kids who believed the show must go on."

"Kind of like Grandma, huh?"

Mom twists her smile into a frown and narrows her eyes when she looks at me. "I just want you to have all the normal things, Boogie. You deserve to have these gorgeous memories of friends and celebrations and secrets and crushes and just...all the regular amazing stuff life has to offer a twelve-year-old."

I lean back in my chair, my heart aching for my mom. "Whatever happened to Jodie?"

"She went on to become a big producer in Hollyweird,"

Dad says. When I gawk at him, he belly-laughs so hard, he shakes the table.

Mom smiles at the thought of it. "She has a sweet family in Naperville, a nice suburb in Chicago. Last post I saw on Facebook was of one of her sons winning an award at a science fair."

"Do you all ever talk anymore?"

Mom looks away and circles back to me. "I just want you to be happy. And I'm just trying to do the absolute best I can at this job. It isn't easy, you know. You need different things than I did, and I need to keep reminding myself of that so I can honor it."

"You're doing a stellar job, honey," says Dad.

"I'm just trying to be a really good..."

"Mom," I finish.

She reaches for me, and I get up from the table and snuggle into her arms.

"So, Superstar," Dad says, wiping his own tears away and unruffling his slouchy tee. "When do you make your big TV appearance?"

"Well." I look up at Mom, who nods approvingly.

"It's your happy to find, Boogie." She looks around the kitchen. "I found mine."

"So, Superstar?" Dad asks again.

I guess now is as good a time as any to be honest about

just how far my happy has slipped away from me. "I'm not guaranteed a spot in the top sixty-four," I admit, shrinking away from them. "I lost my part in the play, so now I'm not qualified to compete."

Mom gasps. "Just when I was ready to see you on the silver screen." She fans herself with her fingertips. "How, exactly, did you lose your part, Boogie?"

I tip-toe out of the kitchen and say, "Long story."

"We have nothing but time, young lady," Dad says as I run up the stairs, taking two at a time.

Mom's words catch me on my way up the stairs. "We still need to talk about your punishment for going behind my back. And for forging my signature."

"K!" I yell down the stairs before heading to my bedroom. Fact: Getting grounded seems like a small price to pay for my big dream. I'm just glad Mom is finally on board with letting me chase it.

CHAPTER 20

Monday morning when I get to school, pretty much all of the sixth and seventh graders are throwing me serious side-eyes. It's obvi that they've seen the Live. The eighth graders don't even bother looking in my direction. My heart aches for all the stars who've fallen from grace after some big scandal. I know how they feel.

"Are you okay?" Twinkie asks, falling in step with me on the way to the theater.

"Georgia is still ignoring me and pretty much avoiding me at every turn. And Mom said the worst thing to me ever: that she's…" I make air quotes and continue, "Disappointed in me."

In one word, Twinkie cosigns that this is the worst thing a parent can say to a kid. "Ugh!"

"She pretty much promised to ground me for my sins. The jury is out on the punishment for now." I adjust my leg warmers. "But other than that—"

"Oh no!" she squeals, fussing with the tight bun on top of her head. "You haven't seen it?"

I stop walking. "Seen what?" Then I look over my shoulder for dragons or aliens or monsters. "What apocalyptic thing happened that's causing you to unravel?"

"Uh, well…uh…" she stammers, slowly inching her phone out of her backpack. She cues something and hands it to me. "Check it out. But at your own risk."

"Twinkie, I really don't have time for this today. I don't know if you've noticed, but I'm sort of a pariah around these parts." I bite my lip, pressing PLAY on the screen.

That's when I see it. Someone remixed my Live into a mashup of auto-tuned words that were exchanged the other day between me and Mr. Reynolds—you know, the day he fired me from the play.

"Who did this?!" I ask, staring at every kid that walks past me in the hallway. "Who. Did. This?!"

"I dunno," Twinkie says, flustered. "It was posted from a Finsta account."

"A fake Insta?" I huff. "The troll doesn't even have the decency to show their face in these Valentine Middle streets?!"

With Twinkie on my heels, I storm off, not bothering to stop at my locker.

"What are you going to do?" she asks, her hands waving through the air.

I squint my eyes and focus on the doors to the theater a few paces ahead. "Get my spot back in the play."

"Oh. Yeah. About that." Twinkie stops walking.

I spin on my suede booties to face her. "What now?"

"Well. They already took your name off the website and put Stormy Jackson's next to the role of Dorothy."

I throw my head back, shut my eyes, and count to five. Brooklyn taught us to do that when we start to feel the walls closing in on us. If these walls get any closer, I swear I'm going to punch them.

"What is happening around here? Has everyone gone mad?" I bend over and grab my stomach. If I wasn't living in my own body, I'd think someone was squeezing my intestines around my belly. I struggle to breathe and try to focus on counting, this time backward from five.

"It's going to be okay, Lyric. Really." Twinkie stands on

her tiptoes to massage my shoulder. "You can always star in the musical next year."

"As if!" I blurt out before remembering that I'm supposed to be the new and improved Lyric Darby. "I mean…that's not really an option, Twink. My time to shine is now."

"Okay then." Twinkie blinks her eyes five zillion miles a minute, bending over to meet my eyeballs. I search the linoleum floor for answers. "What's the plan?"

"I have to talk to Stella Rose; she's the set designer, and she loves me."

"All facts," Twinkie agrees, craning her neck to meet my gaze when I finally straighten. "What are we talking to her about, exactly?"

"I think a good angle would be positioning me as the helper. You know, doing the grunt work and showing Mr. Reynolds that I'll do anything for the sake of the play—even get down and dirty."

"Oh. I get it," Twinkie says, then she shakes her head. "But it's from the heart, right?"

"Yeah." I rest my hand on top of her head. "Of course."

"Okay then. Cool." Twinkie walks ahead of me and opens the door. "We'll go talk to her. But I'll wait out here cuz I'm still not going anywhere near that stage again."

"You really should get your part back, too."

"Nope. This is all about you. Luckily, Stella Rose is a total sweetheart. It'll all work out just fine." She nudges me into the theater, and I head straight for the stage.

"Stella Rose! I need to talk to you," I announce, watching her hammer nails into a slab of plywood.

"What's up?" she asks, not looking up from her project. "Whatcha need?"

"I, uh, want to know if—"

"Oh!" she gasps when she sees me. "It's you."

"Well, I've been me all day," I say, trying to lighten the weighty moment.

She loosens the checkered infinity scarf around her neck and straightens her glasses. "I didn't mean to geek out; it's just that I wasn't expecting to see you standing there...I mean here, in the theater."

"I know, huh?" I shrug. "And yet, here I am."

"What's up, Lyric?" she asks, looking around at all the kids working on the sets. "We're kinda busy."

I inch closer to her and crouch to look into her eyes. Maybe she'll see my soul and give me a break today so I can get this whole thing back on track. "I want to talk to you about coming back."

"What do you mean?" she whisper-asks. "You're not in the play anymore, right? Or did Mr. Reynolds change his mind?"

"It's not about Reynolds," I try to explain. "I know you have a lot going on right now."

"Yeah," she agrees. "It's a bear. And the play is in two weeks."

"I was wondering if you wanted some help. I could take some of the stress and pressure off you. You know, I could maybe be part of…the set design squad."

"Oh," she says, surprised. Then a plain old "No, I think we're good" follows.

"But…you just said you have tons to get done before opening night next Saturday."

"I do. But, uh, I have the football players helping with the heavy stuff, so we'll be okay."

Humph.

"But thanks for asking, Lyric."

I turn to walk away, but then…"What gives, Stella Rose?" I ask, turning around.

"Well." She takes a deep breath and sets the hammer down. "Lyric, you really rubbed a lot of people the wrong way when you called our production amateurish. And to be honest, I'm not so sure set design is the department for you."

My eyes saucer and my belly churns. "Oh."

"The other kids working with me were saying that they're still in their feels about it." She shakes her head.

"They're just kids trying to make something special happen. We know we're not making sets for Broadway, but our little play is important to us."

"I know that."

"Do you?" she asks. "I really look up to you. And so did pretty much everyone else around here."

"But—"

She stands and waves her arm around the stage. "They're all giving their time and energy, trying their best." Her eyes pierce through me, shooting daggers of disappointment. "Your words hurt them."

"But I didn't mean what I said." I try to reach for her, but she steps away. "I thought we were friends, Stella Rose."

"And that's why it hurt so much."

CHAPTER 21

"This redemption thing is going to be harder than I thought," I say to Twinkie on our walk home. Stella Rose is the nicest, most understanding friend I have. If she's not willing to give me another chance, it's beyond obvi that I have my work cut out for me.

"Honestly, I know how she feels," Twinkie says when we get to my front door.

I shift in my booties. "I think I'm starting to get it."

"You're just going to have to show everyone that you learned your lesson."

"Guesso," I say, turning the lock. "You wanna hang out? We can dress up and sing show tunes in the backyard."

"No." She rubs my arm and forces a smile. "I'm gonna go home and catch an old episode of *Big Mouth*." She shrugs and admits, "Today was heavy; I need to laugh." Then she turns and heads home, leaving me alone with all this emotional stuff.

"Hey, Boogie," Dad says when I sulk into the kitchen. "How was school today? How'd Mission Dorothy turn out?"

"It didn't," I admit. "I had a plan to get my friends back on my side and then use them to show Mr. Reynolds that I deserve my part."

"I have a strong feeling that your friends probably aren't into being used."

I shrug and cross my arms over my chest. "I didn't mean it that way, Dad."

"Then how did you mean it?" He grabs an apple from the fruit basket that was delivered from Mom's manager, bites into it, and leaves me to ponder all my stuff. And it's heavy. And complicated. And exhausting.

But he's right.

Two days later, I'm still thinking about Dad's big question. How *did* I mean it?

"Hey, G," I say to Georgia, holding my hand out for her

to join me in our secret handshake. I ease into my seat for homeroom, waiting for her to make eye contact. Then when she does, she just smirks.

"At least she looked at you," Twinkie whisper-confirms over my shoulder. "It's progress."

"So, I've been thinking," I say to Twinkie, swiveling around in my seat to face her.

"Do tell," Twinkie says, leaning in closer. She tugs on her fave traditional faux-sapphire necklace.

"How do you feel about practicing your songs with me after school today?" I hold my hands in the air. "And before you say no, just hear me out."

Twinkie's brows crease her forehead. "Uh. No."

"Just listen. I checked the website, and they haven't replaced you yet. And Stormy can't exactly play your part and my part, too."

I watch her face scrunch into a frown when she says, "Uh-uh."

"I know you're scared, but to be honest, Twink, I don't think they'll find a better Lion." I shrug. It's true. Twinkie was on the verge of crushing that part until—

"Are you actually thinking about coming back to the play?" I hear Buster say, before he bursts into a weird cackle.

"He's so extra," I tell Twinkie, blowing him off. But

when she lowers her head, cowering in defeat, I can't take it anymore.

I pound my hand onto the desk. "Who do you think you are?"

Buster stops guffawing long enough to point to Twinkie and me, uttering, "I'm the Tin Man." He jabs himself, pointing at his chest. "I'm still in the play, that's who I am."

I look around at the other kids who are filing into the room, laughing with him.

"Teasing someone is actually pretty lame."

"Says the girl who got kicked out of the show."

"At least I'm trying to make it right." I walk up to him, and in my deepest voice, I say, "Only cowards bully people."

Buster takes two big steps backward and trips over the desk behind him. A loud shriek echoes across the room, and the class collectively gasps.

"You seriously have to chill, Buster." His lanky body is sprawled across the floor and his face is smooshed against the linoleum. "This tough-guy act you're always rocking is, like, so last season. I think it's past time to end the hate."

I watch Buster roll over and scramble to get up from the floor, but his Crocs slip and slide on the math worksheets underneath his feet. It's just sad at this point, so

I offer an olive branch. But when I extend my hand, he refuses to take it. I look down at him and explain.

"We've all got our stuff, Buster, I get it, but news flash—everyone has something really cool about them, and if I'm being honest, I think you do, too. Maybe try focusing on that and not so much on everyone else. We're all just trying to do our best in this seventh-grade world."

He rolls his eyes, but I keep going anyway. "I don't know your life, but maybe there's stuff bothering you, or maybe you're going through something tough, and that's why you lash out."

I offer my hand again, but he just spews more venom and then snarks at me. "You're right, you don't know my life."

"I literally just said that!" I huff. Then I try shifting gears again. "You don't have to be so stubborn." I lean over and empathize. "I know we might not always get along, but if you ever want to share, I'm here to listen."

"And why would I ever talk to you?"

I shake my hand in his face, still dangling that olive branch. He doesn't take it; instead, he looks around at the kids recording him with their phones. That's when I notice the red dots that are popping up all over his cheeks and chin. I start to feel bad for him; I know all too well how he feels.

"The truth is, I might not be everybody's favorite person

right now, but I stand by the fact that if we all try to be kinder to each other, things could be better around here."

I glance at Twinkie. I know for sure she'd still be in the play if everyone had stayed in their kindness bag—including me.

I reach down and grab Buster's arm and help him from the floor. I'm no stranger to being paralyzed with embarrassment, especially when there's a cell phone capturing it all.

Buster swats at the dust balls on his butt just as Twinkie starts a slow clap. I look around the room at the other kids, who start clapping, too.

"Seriously, Buster, how about you level up from this drama and maybe try a sprinkle of kindness? I believe in you. You can do it."

He turns toward his desk and appears to be at a loss for words. This is new. Trust me, Buster always has to have the last word. But not today. Who knew?

I glance at Twinkie, and she winks at me, beaming with satisfaction. A few other kids smile in my direction, still clapping.

"Everyone, take a seat so we can get through the housekeeping for the day," Ms. Pepper says when she walks into the room balancing an armful of books. "Thank you for the applause, but that's not really necessary."

"Thanks," Twinkie says as I plop into my seat.

"He deserved the truth." I pick up a pencil and tap it against the desk.

"Yeah. He did," Georgia agrees, grinning at me.

Later at my locker, I'm touching up my raspberry lip gloss when I feel a gentle touch on my shoulder.

"Hiya, Lyric!" I turn around to find Stella Rose standing beside me with Lucy's arm looped through hers. "I heard about what you did in homeroom today."

Magic jogs up to us with Brooklyn by her side. They both lean into our small circle and smile. "Thank you, Lyric," Magic says, biting her bottom lip. "He's been bugging me about my dancing since I got cast in the play."

"Sorry to hear that, Magic," I offer. "You don't need that when you're just trying to do your best."

Brooklyn high-fives me, causing her rainbow goddess braids to fall over her shoulder. "Thanks for standing up for all of us."

Lucy blows a purple bubble with her gum. Then it pops all over her mouth, sticking to her upper lip. She peels it off and says, "What you did is making its way around Valentine."

Maybe he'll get the message. I snort back at them, "Nobody deserves that."

"I was thinking the same thing about you." Stella Rose purses her lips and blinks several times in a row. Then she pops her red-and-white-striped suspenders. "And maybe you didn't deserve how I treated you on Monday."

"I get it, Stella Rose; you didn't want to be...used," I admit.

She shifts in her Vans and then she says, matter-of-fact, "It felt weird, but now I see that you're just trying to get back in the show. We want to support that, especially if it means getting Twinkie back, too."

"So...what are you saying?" I ask.

"I'm saying that you can work with me and the set design team...if you still want."

"Uh...yes," I blurt before she changes her mind. "That would be amazy."

"And you can work with the costume team, too," Lucy offers. "We could use the extra hands. So many Munchkins. We're a smidge behind." She wipes the imaginary sweat from her temples. "Okay, a lot behind."

"But you can always catch up," Magic reassures her, patting me on the back. "Especially with Lyric there to help you. Cuz we really need the help."

"Magic is right. And I'll work overtime. I won't let you down." I hold out my pinky finger, and Stella Rose links hers with mine. "Pinky swear."

"Coolio."

"I really appreciate this." The knot in my belly is starting to loosen over my high-waisted denim. "I know I have a lot of bridges to rebuild. And I need to show everyone that I'm here. And this time I won't desert them."

"Better late than never," Georgia says, opening her locker behind me.

I turn around to face her. "G. Can we talk?"

"See you later, Lyric," Stella Rose says as she and Lucy turn to walk away. "We'll all be in the theater."

Brooklyn grabs Magic and says into the air, "Come through when you're done, Boogie."

They disappear into a stampede of seventh graders while I wait for Georgia, not leaving until she finally says, "I think I'm ready."

"Good, because I'm hungry and I need to eat." I hold out my hand. "Lunch?"

"Lunch," she agrees, grabbing my hand and leading me to the cafeteria.

I'm certain of what I need to say to Georgia. *If anyone has the right to not speak to me any longer, it's her,* I think as we head to the salad bar.

"Hey, G," I start, happy that she's here and that she's giving me a chance to make it right. "First of all... I'm sorry." I sit at the table and push my food away.

She sets her bright red cowboy hat on the table, and her brown eyes search my soul. "What, *exactly*, are you sorry for, Lyric?"

"I have a list," I admit, pulling a sheet of scratch paper from my jeans. I made it in Mr. Chang's class. He was rattling on and on about equations, and the only one who seemed to understand him was Brooklyn.

"Well, check you out." She bites into a cheeseburger, ketchup sliding down her face.

"I figured that if you gave me a chance to make it right, I didn't want to forget anything."

I watch Georgia wipe her mouth with a napkin and slurp down Dr. Pepper. "I'm all ears."

"Well. Okay. Here goes." I shake out my curls and smooth the paper with the bottom of my Snapple bottle. "I know I should have shown up for you. I should've been at your appointment with the therapist, especially since I promised I would."

"Facts."

"And if I wasn't going to make it to the appointment, I should have let you know."

"Also facts."

"AND I should've followed up with you to see how the appointment went, especially since I wasn't there."

"All phenomenal facts."

"This is pretty embarrassing for me to say, but I had an epiphany. A revelation, if you will, and, well, I'm ashamed."

"I'm all ears," she says, studying my posture.

My shoulders are slumped, and my head is hanging when I whisper-admit, "I, uh... I realize that I did to you what was being done to me."

"Can you say that a little louder? I can't hear you over the ego."

"I said"—my voice gets louder—"I treated you like Jade Darby treated me."

"Oh... and how's that?"

"I turned my back on you to chase fame."

"BOOM!"

I look at the floor then back up at my girl. "And I'm really sorry. I know how that feels better than anyone."

"Now you're getting it, Darby."

"I really wanna focus on not doing that anymore. On breaking that cycle." I think I see her try on a semi-smile, but I can't be sure. "Soooo... do you think you'll be able to forgive me?"

I watch Georgia take another bite of her burger and say between chews, "But, like... why?"

She swipes at the cheeseburger juice that slides down her chin, still checking me out as I fumble through my apology tour. It's hard for me to just say it. Being vulnerable is *nawt* for the weak. But her friendship means the world to me. *Maybe even more than fame.*

"To be totally transparent, I was being selfish. And only focusing on *my* goals."

"Being a diva doesn't look so good on you, Boogie."

"I've come to realize."

"You completely disregarded the fact that—"

"The fact that you and Twink were the ones who helped me get where I wanted to be, and then I turned into a fame monster."

"An ugly fact."

"The truth is, G..." I reach for her hand. She takes her slow, sweet time easing it toward me. I continue anyway. "You and Twink were just trying to help me achieve my big dreams, and I wasn't showing you the appreciation that this level of friendship deserves." I take a deep breath and realize that Georgia has stopped chewing.

"Cuz there are levels to friendship," she says, not breaking our bond.

"And we're, like, at the highest level."

Georgia smiles and finally swallows. "My favorite fact."

"G, you're one of my closest friends. I heart our friendship."

"Uh-huh," she says, cocking her head to the side.

"I don't know what I'd do without you." I squeeze her fingertips and beg for her to take her rightful seat in my heart. "Can you forgive me so we can get back to the way things used to be?"

"Lyric."

"Do you enjoy seeing me beg? Cuz I'll even get on my knees and plead. I don't care if everyone is watching."

She grabs her cowboy hat and shoves it onto her head. "Okay. Do it."

"Seriously?" I climb over the bench and prep to get on my knees.

She slaps the table. "Darby! What are you doing?"

I swipe the floor with my feet to dust any dirt away before kneeling. "Showing you how much I love you."

"Get up!" She pulls me by my shirtsleeve. "You're embarrassing yourself."

"I'll do whatever it takes to win you back!" I yell to the crowd of kids that are looking.

"Just work on being a good friend," she says, shushing my big fat proclamation.

"I can do that," I assure her—and myself. "I can definitely do that."

CHAPTER 22

The next day, Twinkie and I are sitting on either side of Georgia in the waiting room outside of Dr. Simone's office. This is a very big deal because Georgia finally mustered up the courage to go back for round two, but this time, she was going to be in group therapy, vulnerable with a crew of kids. I had to pinky swear that I'd be by her side every step of the way. Maybe her parentals threatening to take her out of the play had a little something to do with it, too. Whatever her reasons, I decided that nothing would stop me from being here for it—and for her. And, yes, for myself, too. I guess.

"I'm not so sure I can do this," Georgia says as we wait for her group session to begin. I look around the room, checking out a handful of kids who look just like us. Confused. Nervous. Frustrated. And ready to get this over with.

I pat G on the knee while Twinkie tries to rationalize the whole support-group thing. "If you can sing in front of giant audiences that you don't know, it only makes sense that you can talk about your feelings in front of kids you don't know." She shrugs. "Am I right?"

"But that's just it...they're *my* feelings. It's one thing with the therapist, but now I gotta be vulnerable in front of other kids, too. Ugh." She shakes her head, her yellow cowboy hat hovering over her eyes. "Soooo not about this life."

"Be about it today," I say, squeezing her cherub cheek. "You have a big show next weekend that you need to be present and accounted for."

"Oh, look at you, Ms. Committed," Georgia says with a hint of snark. "Who would've thought those words would come out of your mouth? If I'm not mistaken, it was you who ditched me for what? Front page of the *Valentine Middle Gazette*?"

I cup my hand over her mouth to muffle her sarcasm. "No need to look back unless we're checking to see how far we've come."

"And we've come a long way, baby," Twinkie cosigns.

I nod in approval. "Let's just say I learned my lesson."

A girl with dried tears and short choppy bangs is watching me. She's been staring at me for the past five minutes, and I'm starting to think maybe she recognizes me from Insta. I smile at her before turning back to my friend.

"Besides, G, can't a girl get a second chance around here?"

"You, my dear," Twinkie says, smizing with her eyes, "can have all the chances in the world."

Georgia shakes her head and warns me with a very stern grimace. "No. You can't."

"I know, G," I say, snuggling closer to her. "I know."

Dr. Simone opens the door to her office, and five kids file into the room, each sitting in one of the chairs that form a circle.

"You're up," I say to her as she reaches into her pocket and pulls out a toothpick.

"You can do this," Twinkie encourages, watching G shove the toothpick into her mouth.

"But..." Georgia looks around the empty room and then at Dr. Simone. She's standing in front of us wearing a rainbow-colored bow tie with stripes and a crisp white button-up. Her colorful socks are striped, too. I've noticed that it's her thing.

I step closer to the good doctor, twirling my finger around her vibe to let her know "I'm totally here for it."

"Thank you." She grins back.

"Would it be okay if we joined Georgia today?" I ask Dr. Simone. "I'm Lyric Darby, and I have some sticky stuff going on in my life. I could use some support, too."

"OMGGG, are you serious?" asks Georgia. "Like, farealz, you're gonna go in there and talk about your business?"

"Can't think of a better way to show support for you," I say, handing Dr. Simone an insurance card. I admit to her, "My mental fitness game plan could use some strategies, cuz, you know, a girl wants to win at this game of life."

"Well, if she's playing on that team, sign me up," Twinkie says, shrugging. Then she digs into her backpack and pulls out her insurance card, too.

"I see," Dr. Simone says, nodding. "I spoke with both of your parents earlier, so you're all set." She steps back, making way for us to join. "Welcome."

Georgia scoffs, the corners of her eyes creasing. "You two knew you were doing this epic thing with me today?! You planned this?"

"Well, you know," I say, feeling confident about repairing the damage I've done to us. "Levels to this friendship thing, remember?"

"Yeah, the highest," Georgia resolves, her brows still furrowed.

Twinkie sits into her hip. "So, Doc, are you familiar with the Lion in *The Wiz*?"

"Of course," Dr. Simone says. "The Lion is legendary for needing courage."

Twinkie's mouth dips into a frown. "Me." She points her finger over her heart. "All me."

Georgia looks back and forth between me and Twinkie. Shock is still plastered over her face.

I loop my arm through hers. "If you're being brave, then *we're* being brave."

"Georgia? Is all of this okay with you?" Dr. Simone asks. "Just want to check in with you."

"Dude," she says, as if it were her idea. "Haven't you heard that healing is cool?"

Then, just like that, we walk into her office and take the last three seats in the circle that are waiting for us.

Thirty minutes later, I think I'm starting to get the hang of it. Group therapy is basically a chance to share your experiences and get support from other kids who are going through similar stuff.

I lean over to Georgia and whisper-announce, "Now I understand why they call it a support group."

"Lyric," Dr. Simone says, switching the attention in the room to my big mouth. "You were saying you wanted to share with us, too."

I look at that same girl with the choppy bangs. She just finished explaining that she's been dealing with some serious sadness since she had to move schools when her parents separated. It's a double whammy because her whole life has been turned upside down, and she feels alone dealing with it all. I'm starting to think she didn't recognize me from Insta; I was just a friendly face, and she was trying to make a connection.

"I, uh... well, I, uh..."

Georgia nudges me to go for it, and Twinkie offers me a thumbs-up.

"Well, I'm really here to help my friend, Georgia."

"I was under the impression that you needed a little support today, too."

"I don't." I look around at all the kids who've just opened up and shared their challenges. I know I'm being a complete coward, but I'm not exactly excited to share that I've been a self-centered attention seeker and that I've neglected my true friends for fame. I can't even begin to find the words to talk openly about my abandonment issues. Who's going to understand Mom and Dad always being on the road and leaving me with Aunt Jackie? *Seriously? It's embarrassing and... sad.*

"I'll go," Georgia says, saving me. "Take the time to get your thoughts together. I know how it feels to have them all jammed up inside."

"Whenever you're ready," Dr. Simone says back to Georgia.

"Hmmm, I'm not so sure where I should start."

"What about all those jammed-up thoughts?"

"Right," Georgia says, chewing even harder on the toothpick that's she's holding hostage in her mouth. "Good place to start." She takes a deep breath. "It's like I can never seem to settle down so I can think or speak clearly about stuff sometimes."

"I feel that way, too," a boy with a fake nose ring says. "A lot."

Then that whole side of the circle nods in agreement.

"Well. I, uh, think I might have a disorder. At least that's what my teacher thinks. Now my parents think so, too. I guess my friends agree." She looks at me and Twinkie.

"I don't think you have anything except tons of courage," Twinkie says.

"And strength," I add.

"Let's try not to put labels on ourselves so soon," Dr. Simone suggests to the whole group. "At least not until a proper assessment has been done. Even then, I like to keep the focus on solutions, on strategies, and on tools that are designed to help you."

"I like that," I say to her.

"I'm glad, Lyric," Dr. Simone says, straightening her bow tie. "We're not our disorders or our challenges. We're so much more than that."

"I knew I liked you," I say before turning to Georgia. "Okay, I'll go after you're done."

"Deal," Georgia says, grinning. Then she continues. "That's the reason I'm here. I guess I struggle a lot. You know, to sit still and pay attention in class. Or to finish my work at my desk. And yeah." She nods and then exhales. "I can't forget my homework. That's a real struggle, too. Plus—" She thinks for a sec, then she adds, "I get angry and frustrated cuz I can't do the stuff most adults want me to do. Maybe I throw tantrums, too. Mom calls them meltdowns." She whisper-admits, "I'm not really proud of that."

"Same," a girl sitting next to Dr. Simone in a Lincoln Middle School hoodie says. "I'm feeling all that right now. Angry. Frustrated. Annoyed."

Georgia makes eye contact with the girl in the hoodie.

They look at each other knowingly. I see Georgia take a deep breath and release into a shared smile with the girl. Maybe that's the beauty of group therapy.

"It's easier to just zone out and think about other stuff cuz there's always so much happening in my head," Georgia finishes. "Then I try to follow all these different thoughts, and I end up disappointing everyone because nothing gets done."

"I know that feeling," the girl joins in again. "I always lose my keys, and my mom says she can't trust me."

"I lose my keys and my phone and my wallet," Georgia adds. "This just reminds me that I'm a failure."

"Not even close," Dr. Simone says. "But we'll get you some strategies to redirect that stinking thinking."

"These are my third pair of glasses this year," a kid with thick green eyeglass frames says to himself. "So. Yeah. Big loser over here, too."

"No one is a loser," Dr. Simone says before anyone can agree with Green Glasses.

"But that's how I always end up feeling," Georgia says. "The only time I feel normal is when I'm on stage performing."

"My friend isn't a loser," I say to Dr. Simone, matter-of-fact.

"No, she isn't. No one in this room is a loser. You're all here, and that first step makes you winners. But let's talk turkey."

"Wait. I'm a vegan," I explain. "Ish."

Georgia laughs, and then a few of the other kids giggle, too.

"Let's talk... strategies," Dr. Simone clarifies. "What if I told you that when it comes to your schoolwork, there are ways to make it more manageable for you? That goes for your quizzes and tests, too."

"I don't think so," Georgia says. "I'm, uh..."

"You're what?" Dr. Simone waits patiently for Georgia to finish her thought.

"I'm, uh..." Her eyes dart to the floor when she whisper-explains. "I'm failing most of my classes."

"Do you think having more time to take your assessments would be helpful?"

"Maybe. Probably." Georgia taps her finger on her chin. "I mean, I understand the stuff; it's not that I don't know the answers. I'm not the best speller, but I'm not dumb."

"No, you're not dumb. No one is; sometimes you just might need to be taught the lessons differently. Some people learn better by listening. Then some kids learn better by seeing, maybe watching a video or looking at someone demonstrate. Then some kiddos learn better by touching and being involved with the lesson."

The girl who had the dried tears sits up straighter in her chair. "I do better when the teacher shows me and lets me participate in what she's explaining, especially if it's with an activity." She smiles for the first time. "That's why I like science; I'm usually doing stuff, and it makes more sense to me."

"Same," says Georgia.

"But our science teacher only does that when he has extra time," Twinkie adds.

Georgia shrugs. "I don't always get it when he just explains how things work. I need to see it, you know. When I get to experience it, too, that's pretty cool." Georgia scoots to the edge of her chair. "Like when we made the rockets work to show force and motion. I got an A." Georgia pops her collar and winks at Dr. Simone.

"Good job, Georgia." She turns her focus to the circle. "A ton of kids are just like that. Visual, auditory, and kinesthetic learning are options for us all. Studies have shown that everyone doesn't learn the same way, and you all are proof."

I think about each of my classes, and when my

thoughts stop on math, I offer, "Mr. Chang doesn't teach that way. He just puts a lot of numbers on the board."

"Well, let's see if we can't get you some accommodations so you can learn the best way for you."

"More time to take my tests would help so I can focus and not get antsy about the minutes ticking away." Georgia stands and stretches. "Plus, I'd be able to get my thoughts together better, too."

"How about extra help with staying organized?" Dr. Simone waits for an answer, but when one doesn't come, she checks in again. "How does that sound? And a few breaks during class to move around and shake out those hands and feet?"

Georgia shakes out her feet, and two other kids stand and join her. A few seconds later, Dr. Simone sets the clipboard on an end table and shakes out her feet, too.

I watch Georgia's eyes brighten and her shoulders start to relax. I haven't seen her this light in weeks. Then she sighs, admitting, "I really wish I could have some of that extra help at Valentine."

"You can," Dr. Simone says, jotting some words onto her clipboard. "I could even arrange for you to have a peer tutor and more support to make sure you understand the instructions for all your lessons."

"Okay, that's it, Doc. Now I don't believe you," Georgia says, laughing. "Mr. Chang is so over me. He's not going to go for that."

"Wait," Twinkie says, crinkling her nose. "You could really do all that? In school?"

"We sure can. These days there are so many ways to help you succeed. You deserve a shot at being great in this world. I see it in you; with the right support in place, everybody else will, too."

"What about when I'm not at school?" Georgia asks, her eyes wide.

"We can help you master relaxation and focus strategies," she says, matter-of-fact. "I can teach you ways to calm yourself and to focus."

"I need to learn how to do that," Twinkie says. "Cuz I get all tense and nervous, and then I can't get these vocal cords to work."

"It's helpful for so many people in all kinds of life situations." Dr. Simone squares her shoulders and motions for us to imitate her. "Now. We're going to start at our tippy-toes and then work our way up the body. Let's inhale while we tense our muscles, counting to five in our heads. Start with your toes. After you get to five, a big exhale and then relax."

I slip off my booties and curl my toes under the balls

of my feet. "I'm doing it," I say to Georgia, who has her eyes closed and is counting to five on her fingers.

"Same," she whisper-agrees, forcing her eyelids shut.

"Now let's move up to our legs. Breathe in deeply, tense those bad boys, and count to five. When you get to five, a big exhale again and then relax."

Then we do our thighs, our butts, our bellies...all the way up to our eyeballs, remembering to take big, deep breaths and long exhales.

"I feel so much better," Twinkie says.

Georgia checks out her fingertips like she's amazed that they're still there. "And I feel calmer somehow. It's like magic."

"Not magic, but almost," says Dr. Simone. "That'll get you mellowed out so you can focus better. If you need to repeat the process, go for it. After a few tries, it works like a charm."

"I can dig it," I tell her.

"Glad to hear it," Dr. Simone says, leaning closer to our side of the circle. "Now. About that support you mentioned you needed."

"Yeah," I say, glancing at Georgia, who is deep in thought about her new strategies and tools. "I think I'm ready."

CHAPTER 23

I didn't know it would be this hard.

It's taking more than a few megaseconds for me to find my courage. I look around the room and see the other kids staring back at me. A boy picks at his cuticle, and Hoodie Girl yanks at the strings on her ivory sweatshirt.

"I, uh—"

"You can do this, Superstar," Twinkie whisper-encourages me.

Georgia taps the oversize face on her Apple Watch. The shape of her pupils shifts when she leans closer. "I went. Now it's your turn."

I check the big clock on the wall and watch the second hand tick around the numberless circle. Dr. Simone leans back into her seat and crosses her feet at her ankles. I count the stripes in her rainbow socks. When I get to five, she wriggles her feet, causing me to snap out of it.

"It's just that it's kind of personal," I finally share with the group.

"This is a safe space, Lyric," Dr. Simone says to me before acknowledging everyone else. "What is said here stays here."

"My sister says the same thing about Vegas," Hoodie Girl says.

"I don't know where to start," I offer, fidgeting with the purple heart on my glittery press-on nail.

"Anywhere you want. Just like I did," says Georgia, like she didn't fight with dread all day leading up to her sharing time. I guess starting is the hard part, because now she's sitting in her seat like the sharing champ. And TBH, she earned it.

"Okay, well..." Then I think about how it's been really hard for me to focus when I'm at that big house all by myself. So I get in the driver's seat and start there. I make sure to take time for the emotional turns. "Focusing has been hard, mostly because I feel sad." I exhale the fear that's trying to creep in. "And alone."

"Even though you're a viral sensation," one of the kids yelps from his seat. I don't look up to see who; instead, I stare at the creases on my suede booties.

"She's still human," Hoodie Girl checks him gently. I appreciate her.

When no one says anything else, I peek around the circle. It feels . . . safe. It's also good to know that this group of kids is trying to find their way, too. So, I keep going.

"I mean, mainly when I'm home it's hard. I just mostly stay in my room. In bed." Then I stop talking because I'm starting to feel like I've shared too much.

"Go on," Dr. Simone says when I pump the brakes. "You're doing great."

"Yeah, you are," Georgia agrees, supporting me. "Just talk about how you feel about all the heavy stuff."

"Okay." I try not to think but to just feel. Then I say, "So, it *feels* like I'm all alone in the world. Like no one understands. And maybe, well, maybe, it's hard for me to sleep and then I just end up *feeling* angry. At them. Even though I know I shouldn't be cuz they're just doing their job."

"Who?" a boy calls out to me.

"This is her share," Dr. Simone says. "Try your best not to interrupt."

"Sorry," he says right away.

"All good." I nod back. But since I don't want to put Jade Darby and Elvis on blast, I just keep going.

"So, *they* leave and I feel hopeless and sad. And alone." That's when I look up at Georgia and Twinkie and say really fast, "Even though I know I'm not alone." I cross my legs and sit still, trying to make sense of all these big and little feelings. "It's the weirdest thing."

"It's just the stinkin' thinkin'," Georgia reminds me softly.

"Well, it's pretty funky because I cry—sometimes—okay, maybe a little more than that. But only when they leave to go on the road for work." I fight the pricks of the tears. "I feel like nobody…" Then I whisper-admit, "…loves me." A wave of embarrassment shoots up my spine, and I shiver.

"You're doing great," Georgia says, shoving her cowboy hat up her forehead. "All of this helps me to understand better, too."

She only deserves the best part of me. "That's why I acted so ridiculously." It's time to be completely honest. "And maybe because I enjoyed being Instafamous."

"That's all in our rearview now," she says. "But I can see it all clearly."

"I was really craving attention from *them*. And somehow in my mixed-up mind, I thought that all the diva stuff would make them see me. Everyone else, too." I stare at the lines on the inside of my palm until they all blur together. "But mainly *them*."

A few sympathetic sighs float through the air.

"When *they're* gone, it always feels like I'm not important." One tiny tear manages to escape. "Like I don't matter."

"Tell them about your appetite." Twinkie pokes her knuckle into my periwinkle puffy vest.

I glance at her and say, "Whaddo you mean?"

"We know you haven't really been eating, babes." Twinkie turns to Georgia for backup.

"We just thought it was because of all the stress of *American Rockstar*." Georgia's eyes look into mine.

Twinkie bobs her head into agreement. "Or, like, a side effect of being Instafamous."

I sneak a glimpse of the group. I've already shared so much. I shrug it all away. "I don't think any of that really matters."

"It all matters," Dr. Simone says.

They're deep in my business at this point, so I guess one more thing won't hurt. I really want to get to the bottom of what's been happening with me, and if this will help...

I count to five in my mind, and then I mutter, "I guess I haven't really had an appetite either. It happens sometimes when they leave me for fame. And I guess I'm not really sleeping either."

"That's nothing to be ashamed of," Dr. Simone offers before the weight of the room can settle on top of my dark roots. "It sounds like situational depression might be what's happening. When that occurs, losing an appetite happens right along with it. Or gaining a really big one. And some people sleep all the time, and others not really at all."

I arch my brows and feel my head tilt to the side, trying to make it make sense.

"Like I said earlier, I'd have to give a proper assessment, but this is all manageable. With the right tools, you'll be able to feel better. Even more, you'll be in control of your mental health journey."

I peel the purple heart off my nail. "Whenever they leave, I don't feel like I'm in control. Not at all."

"I understand," Dr. Simone says.

"Super same," Hoodie Girl says into a finger snap.

I look around the room expecting everyone to be staring right through me with piercing judgment. But they're mostly into themselves, either looking at their own shoes, their hands, or studying the shades of blue coating the walls. So I take a beat and whisper-ask Dr. Simone, "Is one of those tools therapy?"

"It can be," she says, smiling. "Does that sound like something you'd be interested in?"

I nod, mostly because it feels good to get all this sticky stuff out of my head and off of my heart. I didn't know I would start to feel like this. Sorta...free.

"We'd talk about all the things that are on your mind, working through your challenges and unpacking the heavy stuff that has you feeling this way." I watch her count on her fingers. "We'd also work through sleep strategies and find a healthy eating plan." Her eyes twinkle. "How's that sound?"

I half smile back at her and crack the door to my heart a little. "I'm becoming a fan of meditation."

"I see," she says, leaning into the circle. "And music therapy can be very effective."

"That's right up my alley," I pipe, feeling seen.

"So I heard."

I'm thinking deeply, trying to put stuff in little boxes in my mind so it stays organized. "Situational depression, huh?"

"I'm not sure yet, Lyric," she says. "But it's important to remember, labels don't define us."

"Yeah, I get that, but if there's a name for it then that means other people feel it, too."

"Yes. Millions," she informs me, nodding. "Tons of

kiddos your age are going through exactly what you're experiencing."

"So, basically"—I tap my fingertip on my chin—"that means I'm not... alone."

I look around the room at all the kids dealing with their own mental monsters. There's something comforting about all the support.

"Does it also mean you can give me some of those tools and other stuff, too, so I can learn to—"

"Manage it ALL," Twinkie adds. She turns to Dr. Simone. "You said that this is the place to get that stuff, right?"

"Yes, Saanvi, it absolutely is."

Georgia stands up and stomps her cowboy boot into the carpet. We all watch her throw her fist in the air and declare, "Let's all slay our brain pain!"

I take a deep breath and smile.

"Then we can all have..."

Hope.

CHAPTER 24

Later that night, I contemplate the phrase Dr. Simone used to explain my sticky. It feels like a medium-size phrase to explain all my big feelings. But after listening to her and some of the other kids in our sesh, I'm surprisingly not afraid of it. Depression. Situational depression, to be exact. She explained that it's short-term and is brought on by the stress of everything, particularly Mom being on the road so much. She called it a trigger. Now I want to learn more. I'm pretty sure I'm going to sign up for a few sessions with her to work through my big feelings. I can definitely benefit from some of those extra tools and strategies. And music therapy? Yes, please.

"Are you glad you went today?" Twinkie asks me as we sit cross-legged on my bed nibbling on leftover, cold pizza. *It feels like the longest day ever,* I think to myself, and huff because I know there's still more to check off my never-ending TO-DO list.

"Yeah," I admit. "You?"

"I want to go back, Boogie," she says.

I grin at her because I do, too.

"Have you given any thought to rejoining the cast?" I ask, after all the support she got today. "You know, no one would ever make a better Lion than you."

Twinkie's eyes dart around the room. I can tell that this line of thinking isn't brand-new for her. I imagine she's turned these thoughts over in her head more than a few times in recent days.

"Even though everyone was supportive today, I've been thinking. I'm not so sure I'm cut out for the stage, Boogie." She shrugs. "Besides, I don't want to ruin the show for everyone else. They've been working their butts off prepping for opening night. I'd just mess everything up."

"Why do you say that?" I grab her chin and force her eyes to match mine. "You're an amazy singer. You've got that Billie Eilish thing going, and just when we think we've figured you out, you belt out a Jennifer Hudson run and shut everything down."

"I'm NAWT JHud!" she yelps, blushing. "As if!"

"Have you even heard you lately?"

"Every morning in the shower," she admits, while I fumble through my phone looking for a recording of her singing.

"I know it's in here. I archived it."

"Doesn't matter. It's the weirdest thing. I can do it in person when no one is really around, but something banoodles happens when I hit that stage."

"Lemme see." I grab her elbow and pull her off the bed and down the hallway, straight out the back door. I traipse over the lawn, holding on to her shirtsleeve for dear life. I'm determined to do something good today, and the clock is ticking.

"I wonder if some of what Dr. Simone said could actually work for you up here," I say to her, stepping onto the backyard stage. "C'mon!" I wriggle my finger at her. "Get up here, Eilish."

"But—" she protests, walking up to the stage to stand beside me.

"Nope. Let's do this." I crank the music on the speaker

that's propped downstage. "You were made for this role, and the whole world needs to know."

I watch her eyes shoot down to the shoelaces on her vintage Vans. "But I could never sing in front of the whole world."

I hold up my phone and position it to get a full shot of Twinkie. "But you could sing in front of me. Just little ole me."

She stands still at center stage, watching me watch her. She cocks her head to the side like she's picturing herself doing this very hard thing. Then she huffs. I break out into a wide grin because as soon as the music starts, my little Twinkie peeps out a few notes from that mean ole Lion's signature song.

"Lemme see how mean you can be," I say to her, making circles around her wimpy stance. Then I push a little harder. "Pretend Buster is sitting in the audience."

And just like that, she starts to slowly morph into the fiercest Lion I've ever seen. If I wasn't standing there, I never would've believed it was the same Twinkie that wasn't down to blow the world away with her gorgeous pipes. But by the time the first chorus hits, she's feeling it, like deep down in the nooks and crannies of her soul. My girl is even giving face as she hits the lyrics, pumping her fists in the air. Then she stomps upstage and pounds her foot into the hardwood, wagging her finger at the imaginary audience.

"Buster better watch out!" I yelp from behind the camera phone, egging her on before finally screaming, "Let him know what's gonna happen to him!"

♪♪ *You'll be standing in a draft*
If you don't hear me laugh

She's starting to sound so savage when she sings! And I'm here for it. I watch Twinkie finish the song strong, holding up her fists. I manage to record most of it without missing a punch or a fist thrust or even a crouch into her scary lion pounce.

"That was magnificent, Twink," I rave at her. "You even had me scared there for a second."

"You're just saying that."

I crinkle my nose and shake my head for emphasis. "NAWT. Even."

Her voice is hushed when she says, "If I had your voice and your confidence, I could really make that role something special. I mean, if I could just get over my fears and go for it."

"Can you imagine how many kids have fears that they

need to overcome? If you play this part, you'll be able to show all of them that fear is just excitement turned upside down."

She lets that lil' nugget sit in the air for a minute before she asks, "Where'd you get that?"

I remember exactly where I heard it first. "It's just something Jade told me when I was at my very first audition. I think I was four or five, and I really wanted to sing that big song, 'Tomorrow,' from *Annie*."

"I bet you crushed it."

"If I tell you something, you have to promise you won't repeat it."

She takes a step closer, ready to sip all the tea. "Who am I going to tell?"

"That's true," I agree, sucking in the air around me. "I've never told anyone this before. Just like I never corrected the kids when they started the rumor that I'm a member of Beyoncé's extended family."

"Um." She crinkles her nose and rolls her eyes. "You started that rumor, Boogie."

"Did I?" I blush, dodging her accusation.

"C'mon." Her eyes bug, and I can tell she's not going to let me off the hook. "I'm waiting."

"K." I pop a squat on the hardwood, ready to open up to my friend, who I realize needs a little extra mojo to step into her greatness. She sits directly in front of me and leans closer. "Well," I start, "when I was auditioning for that part, I might have gotten so full of nerves that I... that I... that I peed my pants."

"O-M-Get out of here!"

"Uh-huh. And it really sucked because I wasn't wearing pants."

Twinkie grabs her belly and rolls onto the floor gasping for air. "Lemme guess. The Annie dress? Red and white and frilly?"

I nod, hiding my face from the shame that's still hanging around all these years later. "That's why I was so anti singing in that Annie costume."

"Way tragic," Twinkie says, crawling toward me to rub my back.

"So, you see, we all have our quirks, and this is just that—your quirk. The good thing about those is that you can totally get over them. Just step right over them. Or shake them off and keep it moving. Or just flat out stomp them to death. Kick 'em in the—"

"I get it. I get it." She giggles. "You can stop now."

I plaster on a serious face and let her know the truth. "I just want you to know that you're not alone in this whole fear thing. We've all dealt with fear at one point or another."

"And now it's my turn?"

"Looks that way, friend."

"What about you?"

"What about me?"

"What are you afraid of right now?"

I let my encouraging smile slip into a frown. That's when I admit my truth. "That I'll never be accepted again."

"How do you plan on shaking that off, stomping it to death, and keeping it moving?"

"I dunno."

"Hmmm," she says, smiling. "If I know our L-Boogie, you'll think of something."

I smile right back. She knows me well.

Later that night, I'm in my room snuggled in bed, staring at my Insta. I've raked in a few thousand more followers and am reading through some of what the different cliques of kids had to say about my latest singing reels. I put my phone down when I scroll past more than a few trolls. The comments section has turned into a hodgepodge of both good guys and keyboard warriors.

"Can I come in?" I hear Mom whisper-ask from behind my door.

I shove a pillow over my face. My voice is muffled when I finally answer back. "I guesso."

She opens the door and eases inside. “I know things haven’t been so easy between us lately. But I want to share something with you before you suffocate yourself to death.”

I move the pillow away from my face and watch her sit beside me.

“Everything has been hard lately, not just us, Mom.”

“Yeah. That’s usually the way it works, Boogie.” She moves the big curls away from my face and rubs the side of my cheek.

“I have to admit that I don’t know what it’s like to be as brave as you are.” Then she leans down and kisses me. “You have all this fierce confidence. You know what you want out of life.”

“I’ve been watching one of the greatest to ever do it.”

“You really see me that way?”

“Mom, duh!”

“No. Seriously. Because your dad and I both agree, you’re more talented than I’ll ever be.”

“I just want to be like you.”

“But you’re so much better at being you. That’s what I wanted to say to you.” She pinches my nose and smiles. “I used to do that when you were a baby. You had the cutest freckles in the middle of your face, but you didn’t have a nose. So I kept pulling at it and tugging at it until you grew one."

"That's not true."

She crosses her heart and says, "Completely."

"Well. Thank you for my nose." I touch it, still staring into her round hazel eyes. "And for my voice."

"You know, you're a pretty powerful twelve-year-old. You have a lot of influence over others and how they move in the world."

"I'm *nawt* an influencer."

"But you are. A lot of people look up to you. You might not have meant for it to turn out that way. I know you were just doing what you had to do to get cast on *American Rockstar*. But now, you have all these people on social media watching you, waiting for your next move. And that's a lot of power."

"I never thought of it that way."

"You're growing up right before my eyes, and it's not exactly easy for me to handle. I have to loosen my grip and let you do your thing—let you soar." She nods, studying me like she's approving my face. "It took me some time to realize that you're not Lauren Smith. And you never were. That was my story. And this is yours. I want you to live it loudly. Boldly. Proudly. But, Boogie?"

"Yes?"

"I'll be close, you better believe that."

I've waited a long time for her to give me permission to be me. Lyric Whitney Houston Darby.

"I'm sorry for being a brat," I offer. "I just want my career so badly. I want it for more reasons than you think."

She puts her hand over her heart like she's going to lose it if she doesn't hold it in place.

"I have this thought, just hear me out," I start, ignoring my sea legs. I need all my strength so I can sail into an open and direct convo with her. Dr. Simone strongly suggested that I talk to my mom and share my thoughts. She won me over when she said, "You are your mom's greatest dream come true. You deserve an honest relationship with her. You deserve the mom you want. Give her some grace." Dr. Simone and Brooklyn had both given me that advice. Maybe there was something to it, after all.

"Mom, sometimes I feel that if I have this epic glow-up, this mega moment, and I finally become a star, then maybe...you'll never leave me. That you'll be by my side for all of it, because you'll *have* to be."

"Of course I would be there with you. Not because I'd have to be, Boogie, but because I'd *want* to be. There's nowhere else."

"So, see. That's why I HAVE to be famous. So you'll never leave me."

"Aww, baby. Is that what this is all really about? You wanting me to be with you? And not be on tour? Not be on the road so much for work?"

"We talked about this before. You promised then that you'd be around more. "

Mom holds her head. "You're right." A tear steadies itself in her eye. "I'm embarrassed. I let you down."

"Dr. Simone told me that I might be dealing with situational depression."

"When you were in the group session today?" Mom's voice softens.

I nod.

"Is that how you're feeling? Depressed?"

I nod again. I don't want her to feel guilty about my sticky. But Dr. Simone told me to try to be honest. "Well, sometimes. Yes."

"Then, Boogie, we'll deal with it. I'm sorry you're going through this, but I promise I'll keep working to get it right. I know I work a lot, and I know I've promised before...." She looks away. "I'm so sorry, I get so deep into my work that I don't see how negatively it's affecting you." Then she turns back to me, her eyes pierced with intensity. "You're the priority, Boogie. So we'll deal with it. All of it." She pats my hand. "How's that sound?"

I think of how I have to keep my word to Twinkie and Georgia, too. "I understand. I did the same thing to my friends. I treated them exactly how I hate to be treated. And they gave me a second chance, too."

"Thank you for the second chance."

"Dr. Simone suggested that we have a family session. Just you and me." I tread lightly. I don't want Mom to think that I think there's something wrong with her.

"Is that what you'd like to do?" she asks, leaning closer to me.

"I want to get it right." I nod one last time. "So, yes. I think so."

She wraps me in her arms. "Then that's what we'll do."

With Mom by my side, I feel strong.

"Mom," I start, being my most vulnerable self. "I know I've hurt a lot of people trying to take care of what I needed. I ignored some things that were important to other people. Including you. It's important for me to say sorry."

She bends down and kisses my forehead. "I could've done some things differently, too, Boogie." Then she whispers into my ear. "And it's also important that you hear me say I'm sorry, too."

"So, what happens next?" I ask her.

"Beside therapy?"

My eyes are wide.

"Well, now that *American Rockstar* has you on hold, everyone wants to know how your story is going to end, including me." She gets up and pads to the door. "Why don't you tell us all . . . what's next?"

"As far as my fame, I wish I knew."

"If I know show business, Boogie, and I know show business . . ." The corners of her lips turn up to smile as she opens the door to leave. "This is all just the beginning."

CHAPTER 25

I spend the final week leading up to opening night working overtime to help any and everyone who would give me an opportunity. Every day after or before school, I could be found toiling away with Lucy, sewing Munchkin costumes until my fingertips dripped little pellets of blood. Or I was painting that annoying yellow brick road for hours. I even helped Magic and Brooklyn master their routines in my backyard. Whatever it took to show up and be of service to my friends. Then early Friday morning, I had The Dream.

*   *   *

I wake up and bolt out of bed, heading for the stage in the backyard. I know this is "the lady in the basement reading tarot cards" adjacent, but this wasn't just any old regular schmegular dream. The one and only Whitney Houston appeared right here in my backyard, on this very stage, and delivered a special message—to me! Okay, so maybe that's more along the lines of psychic/medium lady in my living room, but still, it's very on-brand for me. And since she's my singing idol, I paid close attention. What she told me was way harsh, but when Whitney speaks, I listen. After waking up in a sweaty panic (ew!)—mainly because she warned me about the low-vibrational energy I'd been putting out into the world—I got out of bed and struggled to look myself in the eye. Let's just say that's *nawt* on-brand for me. I love me...and since I've been working on *liking* me, too, she told me that I had one thing left to do.

"You ready?" Aunt Jackie says, holding my camera phone as steady as she can.

I'm about to go live.

In my backyard.

"Spin the camera around," I say to Aunt Jackie.

She trips over her blue housecoat as she whirls around and says, "This is for the trolls."

"And my fans to see that I'm going live from my happy place. The stage."

Aunt Jackie counts down on her fingers. Five... four... three... two...

And here we go.

"Grand rising," I greet everyone as they start to file in and join me. "It's me, Lyric Darby, and I'm coming to you today because I need to say something important." I walk downstage to the speaker and turn on the music. It's the song Twinkie sang last week, and I let it blast while my followers greet me in the chat.

I'm not uber excited about opening my whole heart to all the handles in the Live. At first, I didn't mind having people in my mix; it's the price of fame. But when it comes down to my personal stuff, that just makes me itch. But Queen Whitney was right; low-vibrational frequencies just don't hit the same way honest, uplifting, supportive energy does.

So here we go.

When the song ends, I loop it and it begins again. I turn down the volume, take more than a few deep breaths until it becomes awkward... and I finally speak clearly into the camera.

"That was my girl, Twinkie, singing her heart out."

I take the phone from Auntie and try to read a few of the comments that are scrolling up the screen.

"She's the next big thing at Valentine Middle," I say in response to one of them. "She's in seventh," I answer someone else. "She really doesn't know how good she is," I explain. "I'll pin her IG handle so you all can follow her." I type in Twinkie's @ before getting down to the business at hand. "I won't take up too much time this morning, but my spirit told me that it's time to . . . to . . . to live in my truth."

I sit center stage and breathe in courage. And determination. And humility. "I'm not sure if you all know, but I've been auditioning to be on *American Rockstar.* Maybe you saw my video on their page or on their website. For those of you who don't know, I'm competing for an opportunity to make my dreams come true. Let's just say that in the process, I've become someone I'm not proud to call Lyric Whitney Houston Darby."

I summon all the brave girl energy in the atmosphere, but I still stumble over the next few words.

It's more than a minute before I'm able to sort out all the feels that I didn't know were planning on showing up today. I keep going. It's the same as when my pitch is off and I hit a few bad notes.

"TBH, I haven't been my best self. If I'm keeping it a hundred, I've been... selfish. I'm not proud of the version of me my squad has experienced. I've let a lot of people down, and I've even hurt my friends. Truth: I could've been nicer—kinder—to my family, too."

I stop to read a few of the comments as they scroll up my screen.

U turnd N2 a fame

you're SO full of yourself

"I admit that I let the fame of it all get to me." I shrug into the camera, fighting the urge to shut it off and hide. But I don't. I can do hard things.

"It's not easy," I continue. "But I can admit that I went left. I have a dope scout squad and an equally amazing theater squad who have both helped me see how far I've fallen. I'm ready to get back up and stand strong. I did some things to you that I felt were being done to me. I didn't even realize it. But now, I want to be the Lyric Darby the world needs. Well, maybe not the world—but you know what I mean."

I read a few more comments and choose to answer one.

"Yes, you're right, I was a diva." Then I think about it and choose to shed a layer, showing up to my fans and my haters as my true self. "I thought that's how a diva was supposed to behave. I couldn't keep being me. I had to be a bigger, grander version of me. Otherwise, you wouldn't like me. Right?"

It takes a millisecond for them to answer, and I have to agree with every word they type.

"I didn't like me either—so you're not wrong." I flip my curls and hold my head high. "As far as my career, I pinky promise that no matter what happens with *American Rockstar* or with, well... my so-called life, I'm going to bring the most authentic version of me to the stage." I'm about to end the Live when I see a response.

> Im still ur BIGGST fan. I want 2 b just like u. I guess I shld b nicer 2 my friends 2.

"Yes! Kindness is queen!" I snap my fingers into the screen. "I'm sorry for not giving you the best of me." Then I decide to get specific, so they know exactly how I feel. "That goes for Mr. Reynolds and the entire cast of *The Wiz* as well as to you, too, Georgia and Twinkie. And especially Jade Darby, my very, *very* cool mom."

I see Aunt Jackie wipe away a few tears and feel mine

escape, too, without my permission. Then I say, "You deserve better. And so do I."

After school, I head toward the theater, no camera crew in tow this time. I'm barefaced, except the lip gloss that makes my smile pop. C'mon, a girl still has to live. On purpose, I kept it simple: a denim jumpsuit with buttons down the front and black Vans. My oversize sunnies that can usually be found covering most of my whole face are stashed in my messenger bag—along with my ego. I make eye contact with everyone who looks my way and smile. I'm on a different kind of mission today; just like Whitney Houston told me, I'm standing in my naked truth.

"Hey, Boogie!" I hear Twinkie call from behind me. "Wait up."

I turn around and give her a panda-bear hug, almost smothering her little head. "Are you going where I think you're going?"

Twinkie untangles herself from our spiderwebbed hug and stands on her tiptoes to look me in the eye. "You know, I watched your Live, like, a ga*zillion* times."

"I meant every word of it, too."

She smoothes her embroidered pink-and-gold Patiala suit before shoving her hand onto her small waist. "You didn't even tell me you were going to do that."

"It was something I had to do for myself—and by myself," I admit, pulling her long braid from her woven top. "Besides, if I talked about it beforehand, I might've talked myself right out of it."

"I'm proud of you." Her eyes gleam.

I open the double doors to the theater and wait for Twinkie's next move. "I'm proud of me, too."

Her cheeks blush when she looks up at me. "Considering I have a trillion new followers, thanks to you posting my song…"

"Uh-huh, I might've read a few comments they left for you under my post."

"I guess I have a social responsibility to them now to get my part back and give it my all."

"I'd say." I laugh and step back for her to walk into the theater. And she does. Just like that.

I'm glad my little push proved to be enough for Twinkie to realize that she's bananas talented and was basically born to play the role of the Lion. And while I think I'd make the perfect Dorothy, I'm just hoping my old theater squad will accept me again and continue to let me help wherever I can. Baby steps.

"You know, Lyric, I think I could use a cup of peppermint white hot chocolate," I hear Lucy gush from down the aisle. She's fitting the Munchkins in their neon-green-and-yellow costumes and only half-grinning at me. "I mean, since you're here and you're working on being your best self and all."

"Ooh, Lucy, that's harsh," I say. "Even for you."

"I have your video to prove it. With thousands of views, I now have witnesses that all heard you say you're working on helping others. So, to the barista you go."

"I guess you got me there." I shrug and nod in agreement. "If you really can't live without a peppermint white hot chocolate, then I guess I can get a short list together and make a run to Starbucks."

"Good, cuz I could really use a caramel ribbon crunch Frapp," Winnie yells out as she rolls past me in her wheelchair, barely clearing my big toe.

Stella Rose stops taking candid pictures of the cast doing last-minute tech rehearsal stuff to add, "And grab me an iced black-tea lemonade."

"Oookay, lemme write all of this down," I say, plugging in orders to my notes app from Magic and Brooklyn, too.

"I'm feeling a mango dragon fruit," Brooklyn says, and Magic holds up two fingers. They're coming at me fast, and I'm determined to keep up. Whatever it takes, right?

"I have no idea how y'all expect me to carry all this back by myself, but I'll make it happen."

"Wait! I have an order, too," LuLu yips, in a very non-LuLu

tone. I rush to write in her sugar-cookie almond-milk latte just as Buster runs up a tab before I dash out the door.

"Me too! Me too! Pumpkin-spice latte me, please," someone adds to the massive list of requests.

"But we're not in pumpkin-spice season," I say into the thick air.

It isn't until I hear Magic squeak out a laugh, and then LuLu and Winnie giggle-snort, too, that I realize they're all messing with me.

"Are y'all actually pranking me?"

When Buster and Stella Rose belt out a series of bellowing snickers, I know they're enjoying all the funnies at my expense.

"Okay, okay, you got me." I flash a grin, getting in on the joke. "But seriously, now I want a caramel macchiato." But before I can consider coffee, Mr. Reynolds waves me over to him.

"Lyric, can I have a word?" he asks from across the theater. He's standing in front of the piano with Twinkie, who high-fives him and walks away.

"Buster?" Mr. Reynolds bellows for his attention and nods at Twinkie. "Buster, what did we talk about?"

My eyes fix on Buster, who drags his feet, his head down, trudging toward Twinkie. Reluctantly, he extends his hand to help her up the few steps.

"And what else?" Mr. Reynolds says.

Buster balks, but manages to mutter under his breath, "Congratulations. And... I'm sorry."

It's super obvi that it's hard for him to offer this olive branch. I'm wondering what's the deal farealz. That's when Mr. Reynolds makes it all perfectly clear.

"There's only room for respect in Oz," Mr. Reynolds announces.

"Giant ultimatum," Magic explains, walking up to me. "He almost got kicked out of Oz and right back to Kansas."

Twinkie looks at me and shrugs before taking his hand to climb the steps to the stage.

"You're taking no prisoners, I see," I say under my breath as I turn my attention to Mr. Reynolds. "Yes?"

"I want you to know that I saw your video on Instagram."

"Yes, and I meant every word of it, Mr. Reynolds."

"I see."

"No more being absent. No more being late. No more being..."

"A diva!" Stormy Jackson yips as she ear-hustles our conversation.

"Yeah, what she said." I acknowledge Stormy's intrusive, but accurate, accusation.

"That was very big of you," he says with a hint of something in his voice that makes me shove my hands into the deep pockets of my jumpsuit where I can secretly cross my fingers.

"I'm more than open to having you back in the musical," he says, casually leaning against the piano.

"I'd like that," I admit, wondering what will happen to Stormy. I'm sure she'd make a purrrfect Evilene.

"Lyric, I've thought long and hard about this, and it wouldn't be fair for me to take the part of Dorothy away from Stormy after everything that's happened. She's been working so hard on it, too, stepped right up and dedicated herself to the role."

Ouch. That stings, but I don't disagree.

"How about you join the Munchkins? I'm sure they'd love to have you."

Me? A Munchkin? I cough into the air, quickly pulling my hand out of my pocket.

"Seriously, Mr. Reynolds?" *He can't be serious!*

Stormy pipes into our conversation, and I wince when I hear her voice. "I mean, if you think that's beneath you or—"

"Of course not," I recover, determined not to let her see me sweat. "I'd love to be a . . . a . . ." I glance in the corner of the stage at Brooklyn and Magic and LuLu doing an admittedly cute routine, no matter how much skipping around the stage is involved. At the end of the day, if that's what I have to do to prove my commitment to my theater squad, then sign me up.

"Where's Lucy so I can get fitted for my costume?" I say to him, ignoring Stormy and her hefty snark.

"That's the kind of attitude I love to see around here," he says right back to me, scooping his fist through the air. "Glad to have you with us again."

"I won't let you down," I say over my shoulder as I turn to the stage, grateful to be back in action.

"Don't let yourself down," he says, motioning for Lucy to get me into costume. "Tomorrow is opening night. It's the biggest day of the year for some of us. And we're all in this together."

After I'm outfitted, I find Twinkie practicing her choreography in a sea of theater kids. We lock eyes, beaming at each other. More than anything, I'm thrilled for her. She spins around in her Lion's costume and takes a bow. I return her excitement by flipping the collar of my new blue-and-red plaid jumper and flick the pom-pom at the top of my red horned hat. I look down at my striped knee socks and sigh, forcing a smile. At least one of us is going to shine. *Make that two,* I think when Georgia tosses her arm over Twinkie's shoulder.

But I'm not here to shine, I remember. I'm still on a mission.

I cross my fingers and shoot out the most important text of the day to the producer of *American Rockstar*:

> Hey Bailey! Just want u 2 know Im back n
> the play. A sorta smaller role. But I'll be
> on the stage for opening night.

While I wait for her to respond, I close my eyes and click my heels together three times. Then I feel my phone buzz:

> Good job, kid. Saw your Live, b.t.dubs...

I stare at the words on the screen. I analyze each one of them, waiting for them to spring to life and tell me what I want to hear.

But they don't.

That's it. That's all. Bailey never types what I need her to say.

So I text her again.

> Soooooooo am I good? R we good?

She doesn't respond.

Maybe I should explain that I'm a Munchkin, I think.

And if she balks, I can remind her that there are no small roles in theater. Plus, she only said that I had to figure out how to get back in the play. She never said I needed to be Dorothy.

I get ready to explain myself, but then I see the three bubbles. . . .

> Sorry. Busy over here. Congrats, kid. A deal's a deal. Looks like you got the last spot in the top 64. See you for the live taping.

But my knees turn to liquid when I read the words that completely rock my world.

> Be there at 7pm TOMORROW NIGHT!

CHAPTER 26

Confession time. I have to admit that I spent a large chunk of the day going back and forth in my head about how to handle this career sitch that somehow turned into a version of middle school Hunger Games. *It's NAWT an easy decision,* I think, carefully considering the outcome of both. I even prayed to Whitney Houston, because a girl needs the voice of angels on her side. Even though I feel like the big people in charge are testing me. I've spent my entire life waiting to get to this point, to the shiny stage with the celebrity judges that I absolutely LOVE! The winning prize is amazeballs. Last season, the boy who was crowned *American Rockstar* opened up for Girl Power on their national tour. And, yep, it was sold out! SOLD OUT.

I stand up, staring back at the girl in the mirror. She's come so far to have it all taken away. Again.

I inhale wisdom and courage—and make my life-changing decision.

"Boogie! It's time," Mom calls from downstairs as I shove a bunch of stuff into a camo duffel. "You can't be late."

She's right. I can't be late for the day I'm scheduled to step into all of my fabulous tomorrows.

"Go get 'em, tiger," Aunt Jackie says as I bound down the hall. "You figured out that a phone booth is no place for an elephant."

I high-five her and say, "And goldfish don't belong on bikes, Auntie."

"That's my girl," she says as I rush off, making my way to the kitchen, craving a box of animal crackers this time.

I stop in my tracks when I see that Mom and Dad have decorated the room with balloons and streamers. They even hung a big sign over the island that says:

CONGRATULATIONS!

"Whoa. Whose birthday is it?"

"Your mom and I both want you to know how proud of you we are," Dad says. "We couldn't have asked for a more special daughter."

"Sweet.com, Dad," I gush. "You're going to make me cry off my lash extensions."

"You look beautiful," Mom says, smothering me in love. She hired a makeup artist to come to the house and doll me up for my big night. "Well worth the headache of getting Gianni scheduled. My superstar deserves nothing but the best, especially on the biggest day of her career."

"I appreciate all the attention, you two, but you don't have to do any of the frilly stuff. It's just a night, like any other night," I lie. They know I'm not telling the truth when my cheeks flush fuchsia and little sweat droplets pop up around my threaded eyebrows.

"You've waited your whole life for this moment, Boogie," Mom says, wiping away a tear. "I know I haven't always been supportive of you taking the next big step on your journey, but I need you to know it's just because I love you so much and I wanted to protect you for as long as I could."

"Your mom has only wanted the best for you," Dad says, getting choked up. "And me too."

I reach for his hand and interlock my fingers with his.

He's always tried to be my secret weapon in this life thing. "I know. And I love you even more for that."

He sniffles into the air. "Your career is going to take off, and you won't be our little Boogie anymore."

"Is that what you've been afraid of all this time?" I turn to Mom. "That I won't be your baby?"

"Maybe," she says, looking away to stare at the stash of brownies on the island.

"I'll always be your baby. Who else would even want me?" I joke, causing Mom to smile. "I mean...have you *seen* me in the morning before my macchiato?"

"The whole world is going to want you. Everyone will be bidding for a piece of you, honey. You're magical." Dad battles with his tear ducts. He's losing. "And we know it."

Mom wraps her arm around me. "And soon the rest of the world will know it, too."

That's my hope. And her fear.

Mom and I hop into Dad's Jeep and head down the street to turn onto Wilshire. It's my favorite time of day, when the sun has peaced out and the air turns a shade of blue that feels electric. I'm vibing with the pulse of the night and ready to make the little girl inside of me proud; after all, she deserves this.

My phone buzzes, and I see that it's Twinkie hitting my line:

KNOCK EM DEAD TONIGHT

I marvel at the beauty of the night as we drive up to Valentine Middle.

I text Twinkie back:

SEE U SOON. LUV, YOUR FAVE
MUNCHKIN

We pull in to the parking lot, and everything is so sparkly. I look around and am certain that I made the right decision.

There was no way I was going to let my theater squad down again. Earlier today, I texted Bailey to let her know that I wasn't going to be able to make the live taping of *American Rockstar.* She texted back:

SMART MOVE, KID. SEE YOU NEXT
YEAR!

I open the theater doors, and people are everywhere. It feels like the whole town came out for opening night of

The Wiz. I wave at Georgia's and Twinkie's moms before making my way backstage.

"No more selfies and ussies," I fuss at Mom and Dad. "Your fans are waiting for you." It's true, a small line was forming to get a pic with two-thirds of Love, Jade. That was a good distraction, because I only have a few minutes to get my hair and makeup approved by the glam team and still be on time for curtain call.

"We need to get you into costume," Lucy says, barreling up to me, as Mom and Dad squeeze in one final goodbye hug. "You're late!"

I check out all the action backstage and allow myself to feel all the feels.

"Lyric!" Brooklyn and Magic call out to me, waving their hands in the air like a pair of octopuses. They're practicing their choreo in a tight space in the wings.

"Break a leg," Brooklyn says, making a hand-heart over her chest.

I return all the love to my friends and know without a shadow of a doubt that I can start trusting myself again. It's cool that I'm not the star of the show, although I don't plan on playing the supporting character for the rest of my life. Tonight's all about the squad, and I'm just honored to be here.

"Thirty minutes to curtain," Winnie directs me, rolling by in her chair. "Thirty. Not thirty-five, not twenty-five, Ms. America," she clarifies, eyeing me with a half smile.

"Thirty!" I yell at the back of her strawberry curls that are pinned into a messy pony. "Got it, chief."

"And welcome back," she says over her shoulder, rolling to the other side of the stage, where Stormy Jackson is holding court.

"Boogie!" Twinkie says, from behind me with Georgia beside her. "This is so amazy!"

"Facts," I yell back.

I move closer to Georgia and put my hand on her shoulder. "I'm really happy to be doing this with you tonight." Then I put my other arm over Twinkie's shoulder. "And especially with you."

"We've all been through a lot to get here," Twinkie says.

"But, TBH, I wouldn't want it any other way," I admit.

"Don't you miss being on the big stage with the lights, cameras, and all that television action?" Georgia asks, sitting into her hip. "I mean, you're giving up your big chance to get in front of the celeb judges, espesh Girl Power."

"I'll catch them next year," I reassure her. "I'm right

where I'm supposed to be, with my theater squad getting ready for the biggest performance of our lives."

For the next thirty minutes, backstage turns into a circus. I poke my head out of the dressing room and see a cast of kids running around, yelling for glam, costume adjustments, and content for their IG and TikTok reels.

A madhouse—and I love it.

I tiptoe to the curtain and peek around to see a full house. My eyes roam the rows searching for my peeps. That's when I spot them, Mom and Dad, sitting in the middle section, just left of center. They said they were just as proud and excited to watch me dance and sing with the Munchkins as they would've been to see me perform as Dorothy.

"Two minutes! Two minutes to curtain!" Winnie yells. "Lyric, get away from the curtain!"

"Yes, ma'am," I answer back, and ease away from the yellow brick road, turning right into Stormy. She's fussing about her costume being too tight and her shoes squeezing her bunion.

From the side of the stage, I can see the house lights dim and hear a wave of "Shhhhhh" spread across the theater. Aunt Em and Uncle Henry scoot onto the stage and take their marks, right before Winnie rolls up to them with the cutest Westie perched on her lap.

"This is Cuddles. Cuddles, meet Dorothy," she says, introducing the pup to Stormy, who sneezes.

"Bless you," I yell to her, and wave at Cuddles like he can see me.

"It's a different dog than the hypoallergenic one we talked about." Winnie shrugs. "That dog hasn't stopped pooping since this morning. So the trainer brought this one."

And then Stormy sneezes again. "AHHHHH-CHOO!"

When Winnie hands the dog to her, she fumbles it, sneezing AGAIN. "AHHHHHHHHH-CHOO!"

Uh-oh.

In that instant, I take a pretty good guess that Stormy Jackson is allergic to dogs. Who knew?

"When you put him down, Stormy, he'll run off the stage to his owner, just before your opening line. All you need to do is hold him for, like, two seconds." Winnie winces. "It's only for two quick secs, K?"

"Gotcha," Stormy says, super nasally, between several more sneezes. "AHHHH-CHOO!" Then something awful happens: She starts wheezing.

"Sixty seconds," Winnie says, and rolls offstage, right past me. "Just get through the opening and send him on his way. Can you do that?" she yells over her shoulder at a very compromised Dorothy.

"AH-CHOOOO!" Stormy nods, throwing her thumb in the air, not able to talk this time.

"How's she gonna get through her songs?" Winnie fusses, searching around for answers.

When she looks up at me quizzically, I smile down at her. "Hi."

She grabs my Munchkin romper and pulls me down to her eye level. "OMG, Lyric!" Her pupils are rounder than our last full moon.

Before she can say another word, the curtains rise, and Stormy turns to the audience with the biggest "AHHHHHH-CHOO!"

"We'll have to pull her off the stage," Winne says, just as Stormy loses her grip on Cuddles. Our mouths hang open as he flies from her arms and races downstage, scurrying for the steps that lead him straight into the audience.

His owner runs from the wings and onto the stage, searching the crowd for him.

"He's over here!" a man yells from the sea of people ooohing and ahhhing at the unscripted turn of events.

"Now he's over here!" A lady stands and points into the aisle.

"Cuddles! Cuddles!" his owner coos, trying to get him

to return to his loving arms. But Cuddles has other plans. If I didn't know better, I'd think Cuddles was trying to make a run for it.

Auntie Em and Uncle Henry stare at each other, confused. But Stormy races off the stage, straight over to... me!

CHAPTER 27

"AH-CHOO!" Stormy sneezes loudly, causing her to rise onto the tips of her sequined red shoes. Then she scratches her throat and digs her finger into her ear to scratch that, too. "I think . . . I think . . . we need to talk."

"Uh, hi, Stormy," I say, looking around for Kleenex or toilet tissue or something.

It's as if Winnie is reading my mind, because she rolls away with a quick "I'm on it."

The curtains fall, settling on the stage, and Auntie Em and Uncle Henry both shrug before padding into the wings.

I turn around to Stormy, stepping back when she snorts up a gust of air like she's about to sneeze it right back out again. "You and Cuddles didn't catch a vibe, huh?"

"It's come to my attention," she starts, waiting for the doggie dander in her nose to settle, "that you've been quite apologetic about your diva antics this semester."

"It wasn't my finest moment," I admit.

She tilts her head and checks out my Munchkin costume. "No. No, it wasn't."

"I really want you to know that my apology tour included the day you heard me and Zain talking."

She smoothes her blue-and-white dress with one hand and grips the little basket in her other hand for dear life. "You mean when you called our life's work amateurish?"

"That would be the day," I continue, hoping she understands that I'd take it all back if I could.

"Well, I saw your Live, too." She purses her lips. "It seemed pretty heartfelt."

"It was." I step closer and try to help her understand. "Listen, I understand why you wanted me canceled. That's what it took for me to learn some really big lessons, so I'm here for it."

"You were acting brand-new, Lyric."

"True. But I didn't mean for you to get caught in my

stuff. And I'm sorry." I flick the pom-pom dangling from the end of my hat with my fingertips. "I'm just happy to be here as Munchkin number seven."

"You were all about that *American Rockstar* life. So, I gotta say I was surprised you were willing to be a team player and perform with the Munchkins."

I pop the too-tight suspenders holding up my baggy pants. "There are no small roles."

"No. No, there aren't." She steps closer to me and takes the deepest breath before saying, "But there's only one starring role. And it looks like I need your help with it."

"Well, if you're asking me to stand in for you and play Dorothy, I'd be honored."

"Oh, good," I hear Mr. Reynolds say from behind me. "I was hoping we could work this all out quickly." He steps between us and reassures Stormy. "It would be just for tonight. We're already working on another dog for you tomorrow, Stormy. One that won't have you sneezing your head off."

Stormy offers me the little basket, struggling a little to hand it over. Our eyes lock and she finally lets it go. All of it.

"Thank you," she says. "I'll never make it to intermission, and I know you'll make Valentine Middle proud. You're an amazing Dorothy."

"It's your part; you earned it. But just for tonight, I'll rock it out for the both of us," I say as Winnie rolls up to us, shoving tissue at Stormy. Then she turns to me, tugging at the arm of my polyester costume. "Great! Let's get you to wardrobe and get this thing off!"

"Thank you, Lyric, for being here," Stormy says, and sneezes her way backstage.

I turn to the cast, who are all watching, waiting to see how the play will be saved. Lyric Darby, reporting for duty. If only for one night.

CHAPTER 28

"Lyric Darby!" three members of the glam squad yell at me. "Lyric Darby!"

"That's my name!" I toss my hands in the air and twirl around. "Where do you want me?"

"This way!" the hair guy fusses, spritzing and spraying my hair that had been matted under the Munchkin cap.

"No! Over here." Lucy puts her foot down, tucking a backup Dorothy dress and shoes under my arm. "Try this on!"

"Okay, but where's my dressing room?" I fake-snarl, in my most demanding tone.

Lucy stops mid-stride and whips her green hair around. "Are you serious right now?!"

"Nope. JK, JK," I say, ribbing her in the side.

Not even five minutes later, the curtains are ready to rise again for a major second try at this opening night thing.

"Break a leg," Twinkie peps.

"Yeah, what she said," Georgia agrees, rocking back and forth on the balls of her feet.

While Stormy recovers with Benadryl and Kleenex in the dressing room, I'm standing in the wings ready for my cue for round two.

It took some unique twists and turns for us to get here, but I'm beeeeyond grateful to rock the red shoes. I turn to Winnie and Mr. Reynolds.

"I'm ready."

Winnie hands off Cuddles, and I watch the Munchkins, Auntie Em and Uncle Henry, and Georgia, Twinkie, and Buster hold their breath—waiting for a sneeze or a sniffle. But all they get is a smile.

"Let's do this!" I wink at them all just as the curtain rises.

The thespians at Valentine Middle launch into the hottest version of *The Wiz* that Santa Monica has ever seen. At least I imagine it to be that way, especially because at intermission, Mr. Reynolds announces to the cast and crew that it is "the hottest version of *The Wiz* that Santa Monica has ever seen."

"You're especially a wonderful Dorothy, Lyric," he finishes. "Thank you, again, for showing up and for being ready." He wipes his forehead with a checkered handkerchief and smiles. "You're a real pro."

"Thank you, Mr. Reynolds," I say back to him. "I appreciate the opportunity to work with such a talented team. I just hope I'm making everyone proud."

"And then some," he says, right before the curtain rises again for the second half of the show. And off we go!

Twinkie crushes her big songs, and Georgia finishes strong. Buster even brings the house down.

"You ready for your big number?" Twinkie whispers to me onstage as we finish the last scene of the play.

"As ready as I'll ever be," I say, waving to Adderperle as she leaves the Lion, the Scarecrow, and the Tin Man onstage with me. I focus on my motivation and say my line, "You mean, that's all there ever was to it? Just clicking my heels three times and I'm home?"

She nods her head and says through her lion's mane in her best Lion's voice, "Ain't that something, Little Mama. I guess it's about time to go home, huh?"

Then Georgia the Scarecrow adds, "Just think, you coulda gone back before you even met me."

I turn to Buster, waiting for the Tin Man to say his line. "Yeah. Before you even got tied up with any of us. Honey, what a shame."

I watch my friends onstage, old and new, and I think to myself that the next line couldn't be any truer. When I say it, I think back over the last month, and I wouldn't change a thing.

"No! It wasn't a shame. Cause if I'd gone back then, I never would have known if you got your heart...and I wouldn't have seen you get your brains, and you, you..."

Then Twinkie turns to me and says in her best Lion voice, "Dorothy, do you really have to go?"

Then I break out into my favorite song of all time. I close my eyes, the words dancing around my heart.

♪♪ *When I think of home, I think of a place...*

And I turn to the audience and lock eyes with Mom.

♪♪ *Where there's love overflowing.*

Halfway through our signature song, I motion for the music to continue, and I wave for her to join me onstage.

"You're doing amazing," she yells out over the pulse of the crowd. She stands, her hands over her heart. Then she bows down like she's giving all the praise. I feel tears prick my eyes when she blows a big kiss with both hands and announces, "All on your own."

And I finish singing.

The crowd stands on their feet, swaying side to side. Then one person in the theater turns their camera light on me, and then another, and then by the time I get to the end of the song, everyone in the audience has their phones in the air, shining the light brightly on me.

I hold the last note, using all the air in my belly. The crowd applauds so loudly that I almost missed the hooting and hollering happening in Mom and Dad's section. I take a bow and do my best to hold on to this feeling for as long as I can.

"Lyric! You were sooo good!" Twinkie says when the curtain closes. "Like. Ohmahgawd!"

"I couldn't agree more," a woman's voice says from behind me.

"Thank you," I say, spinning around to see Mom and Dad standing with an older woman wearing bright red lipstick over her smile. She nods at an older gentleman holding a cane.

"Lyric, honey, they're from the Fab Kids Talent Group," Dad explains.

I hold out my hand and formally introduce myself. "I'm Lyric Whitney Houston Darby."

"Such a big name for a big talent," the woman says.

The man pounds his cane into the floor. "That's exactly why we're here."

"I'm all ears," I say as Mr. Reynolds tosses me a thumbs-up, snaking through the thick crowd.

"Well, that was quite an outstanding performance you just gave," the man says. "We'd love to see more of you."

"I don't have anything else booked. I mean, I'll be doing *The Wiz* for the next two weekends, but you've already seen that."

"We think we have an opportunity for you," the woman says. "We'd like to send you out for the role of Tinker Bell."

"What does that mean? Send me out?"

The man takes out a business card. "We're a talent agency, and—"

Mom looks down at me, her cheeks rounding as she smiles. "What they're saying is that they'd like to represent you—as one of their clients at Fab Kids."

"Like an agent? An actual talent agent?" I screech, dizzying.

"Yes, and one of our production partners would love you."

"As Tinker Bell? The one and only Tinker Bell?" I shake my head, all of it starting to register. "I just saw Tinker Bell onstage this summer."

"I think I should explain," Mom says.

"There's usually a catch," I say to the woman, who's still smiling. I finally get it when she puts her hand on my shoulder and explains.

"Lyric, this is for a major motion picture."

"O-M-Goodness! You mean, like, a... movie?!"

"Now I think she understands," Dad says to them.

"That's my dream," I announce to everyone. "My whole, entire dream."

"That's right, Boogie," Mom says. "It's time."

Twinkie and Georgia wave at me. I manage to wave back, counting down the seconds until I can share this epic news with them.

The theater is abuzz with Valentine Middle energy—and I know my life will never be the same.

Mom turns to me and softly sings the final words of our signature song. And then I click my heels three times, finishing it with her.

And finally, it feels like... *home.*

ACKNOWLEDGMENTS

Thank you, Timothy Shannon Johnson, my rock, for always showing up for me and for us. You make life sparkle.

Thank you to my mom, Blondie, for never giving up on the possibilities. You, my love, are golden, and I'm a very lucky girl.

Thank you always to the unbelievable team that keeps this middle grade machine on track. I have the absolute best agent, Marcy Posner, who stands beside me, making magic happen. Always looking forward to the wild ride with you.

My beautiful and patient editors, Lisa Yoskowitz, Samantha Gentry, and Alexandra Houdeshell, you all are pure literary dreams.

And this book cover…just WOW! The art team behind my gorgeous covers, Gabrielle Chang, Jenny

Kimura, Karina Granda, and Yaoyao Ma Van As, are brilliant. Thank you for always, *always* getting it right.

A special thank-you to the behind-the-scenes teams who work tirelessly for their authors.

Thank you, Cassie Malmo, for putting me in all the right places. And thank you to Marketing and Sales as well…because of you our girls can continue to read their stories and pass them around like the special gifts they are.

Lastly, thank you to my family and friends for sitting front and center for all my dreams, big and small—especially my Sisky, Kristy R. Goodwin, who tirelessly breaks stories with me like it's her day *and* night job.

I love you all forever.

Timothy S. Johnson

ERIKA J. KENDRICK

is a national speaker, mental health advocate, and former NBA cheerleader. She is a Stanford University graduate with an MBA in marketing and international business from the University of Illinois. She is the author of *Squad Goals* and *Cookie Monster.*